The Matilda

Jon Gray Lang

THE MATILDA

Cover Image by Tithi Luadthong

ISBN 978-1-7323305-0-4

Library of Congress Control Number: 2018911292

Jon Gray Lang

To Amy T., thanks for inspiring me to get this done.

Jon Gray Lang

THE MATILDA SERIES
The Matilda
Twistin' Matilda
Black Matilda
Secret Matilda
Waltzing Matilda

Also, by Jon Gray Lang
Nun with a Gun: Town with No Name

one

Boney was a Warrior

The pilot of the trawler, Matilda, let the ancient craft drift slowly through the vacuum of space. A vast, gloomy emptiness surrounded them with nothing but motes of dust for company...

Drifting... Dreaming... Dreaming of the past... Remembered days of working aboard the tug ship at her home asteroid... Slowly maneuvering the recently mined rich ore to the refinery holding pen for processing later... My first true job on a ship...

It feels like millennia ago. Simpler days those, in many ways. Working to make enough to feed me and mine. All lost now... Lost to time...

"Why do these old memories haunt me now?" she wondered.

Luli sighed as she opened her eyes

Jon Gray Lang

and pulled Matilda's screen visor back into place. She reached for the wires that trailed loosely from the back of her skull, then hesitated.

"Better to stay alert for now. Plenty of down time depending on how this goes." She returned to the visor and perused her star charts for a final time.

***

The Captain floated slowly down the main shaft from the onboard gym to the engine room. Strands of black hair floated in front of her golden eyes as her fingers traced the painted figures on the walls in passing. Most of them were faded and chipped, but many of them still held a memory of her time aboard Matilda... aboard home. Happy moments in many ways and yet tinged with a sadness she couldn't... No, she refused to forget.

A growl escaped her while she pulled herself to the hatch of the engine room at the very tail end of the ship, "But we are going to rescue someone this time. We just have to trust in that damned jump engine."

Jacquie stepped through the entryway, her feet clumped to the decking from the heavier than normal gravity. She watched her stocky engineer, Barney, as he stared resolutely at the jump engine. No one knew where it had come from.

She pondered mildly, the same with Matilda for that matter. It was an unknown model from any of the known systems of the Consortium, but she was obviously old military hardware. Her solid design meant she had been built as a workhorse and had performed as such long before she came to be in the hands of the Delahaye family. Human built, without a doubt. The language in the manuals was clear, for all practical purposes, yet there was something about it that was still obtuse, like a poorly done translation. The Matilda was most likely from one of the colonies that weren't part of the Consortium. Probably started by other sleeper ships that Luli liked to tell stories about.

Even accepting that the ship was a design from an unknown human colony, that jump engine just didn't belong. It was alien, uncomfortable. The space around it always felt weird and unnatural. It made her skin crawl. She didn't know how Barney could bear to be near it, but then he had been part of Matilda's crew long before anyone else on board, even before her birth aboard this boat.

"Jacquie, I'd been wondering when you were going to come down here. Are you sure you want to do it this way?" Barney said as he looked up at her.

"I can't think of another way that has as high a success rate, can you?" she replied.

Barney shook his head, "No, not really. Well, she's ready to go when you are." Mumbling to himself, "Wish I'd never figured out how to make it work."

Jon Gray Lang

"You know that's not true, Barney. You would still be poking and prodding at that thing to make it work. In fact you still are." Jacquie made a motion to the hatch, "Anyway it's almost time to meet up with the others. Might as well head back together."

"True enough, true enough," he muttered as he followed her down the shaft.

***

A tall man with a dark complexion and a runner's body disconnected the call he was on as the Captain and Barney arrived in the lounge. Jacquie nodded in his direction and he got up to join them at the large table.

"Are we all squared away, Derain?" asked the Captain.

The bounty hunter nodded as he straightened his lightly wavy hair into a tight queue. Luli came in moments later with her data pad in hand. She plugged it into the table and brought up the star charts for the crew.

"If it isn't our illustrious deep space pilot. When are you going to dump all your charts into the ship's database and save us from this archaic method?" Derain asked somewhat jokingly.

"What? And give away all my secrets? A pilot is only as good as her charts!" She winked, "And my charts are not for you. You couldn't go to most of those places anyway." She shifted her gaze back to the team, "I've already plotted a course for the jump to drop us almost right on top of them." She indicated the two points on her star chart. "They shouldn't see us until it's too late. I've got a confounder loaded and ready to launch as soon as we enter their space. It ought to cut off their external communications and silence their sensors." A smirk decorated her lips briefly, "It should be enough to blind them for as long as we need."

"I love the confidence," Derain said dryly. "As long as everything goes off without a hitch, you mean."

"Well, that's why you're here, isn't it Derain?" Jacquie retorted.

"Of course Captain, of course," he replied drolly. "If I may?"

Luli nodded and disconnected her data pad so that he could connect his. He pulled up a schematic of the target ship for everyone to see.

"As you can see from the layout, it's a pretty standard military frame, nothing out of the ordinary. The plan is to enter the ship mid deck and have Luli lock down the positions of the two targets. We move to extract them and we're out," Derain concluded as he unplugged his data pad and sat back.

"Everyone knows their roles, correct?" There were 'aye Captains' all around. Jacquie brooded momentarily, "This big a job and we are so few. But we can't afford to fail."

"Okay. As Derain said, we're looking

for two people. We have a pretty solid idea as to the location of at least one of them." She looked everyone in the eye, "Just as we practiced, we split into two groups. Barney and I will go after Rabbit. You two will go after Derain's fugitive. The bonus is just about everyone on board should be in cold storage, so guards should be minimal. We'll have the element of surprise; it should be cake."

Luli quipped, "I love cake."

"More reassuring words were never spoken," Barney reflected.

"Is everyone prepared?" Jacquie asked. She wondered if everyone would come out of this in one piece. "We jump in a little over an hour. Grab your gear and meet up in the hangar."

The Captain left the lounge. Barney got up and headed for the lift to get back down to the engine room. Derain left to check his gear one more time. Luli walked back to the bridge and jacked back into the ship's systems.

two

We're Bound for Botany Bay

All four of the crew stood in the depressurized hangar, secured to the walls. It was a large weightless environment and since the jumps from the bizarre engine tended to be violent, they were strapped in for safety. Each of them was armed with a long knife and had a pistol strapped to one leg. They had never done a jump without anyone on the bridge before and fear was thick in the air. Everyone knew that success had to happen or there was nothing to come back to.

"Three, two, one and jump," Luli triggered the maneuver. They all doubled over during the jump as the Matilda crashed into the 'other space' as they had coined it. It wasn't normal space and it wasn't reached by a standard worm hole. Everything about this space felt wrong. The colors

Jon Gray Lang

changed to ones that the human eye shouldn't be able to see. Even the air in their suits was affected as it took on a metallic scent, like copper mixed with earth and overripe fruit. It didn't always smell the same, but the coppery scent was always there.

"At least there aren't any of those scraping sounds, like something's trying to get in. Thank goodness for short jumps," joked Barney.

They all jerked in their restraints as the ship teetered back into normal space. The Matilda was far enough out that it shouldn't trip the defensive guns on their target ship. The deck rumbled beneath their feet as the confounder launched. Their headsets screeched as the confounder kicked on, but then it cleared. As they unbuckled themselves from the wall, Derain opened the hangar doors. The four of them floated to the outer deck and waited for a magnetic lock. All of their eyes zeroed in on the lone ship, the Vogelgesang, as it plowed slowly parallel to the Matilda.

She was a beat-up prison ship. In her better days she had been a light destroyer. They could barely make her out in the available star light, just a darker shape in the blackness of space.

Getting over to that vessel was the trickiest part of this job. Even with their attitudinal jets, if they were off by one degree, they were lost. As one, they all pushed off the deck toward the vessel. They stayed linked together as they floated through the blackness. When they neared the ship, static from the confounder grew louder on their comms. Jacquie spied three men in spacesuits plodding along on the hull of the ship. She pointed them out as she drew her long knife. Derain and Barney followed suit while Luli kept her hands on the controls to the jets.

Their anchor boots were primed and locked onto the old hull. Luckily, it was just a short haul to an airlock. Luli located the airlock controls, connected her external jack and proceeded to bypass the security software to gain access. One of the space suited figures spotted Luli and signaled to the others. Jacquie and Derain spread out. As one of the guards warily approached Luli's kneeled figure, the Captain came up to his side and cut the air hose. The man scrabbled at the hose as Jacquie pushed him forward. His magnetic boots detached from the hull and he floated out into space. As she turned her head, she saw another man float by, his air venting into space. Derain and Jacquie moved toward the third man as one when a small puff appeared in the man's faceplate and atmosphere started venting out. Barney dropped his wrist to his side and gave the Captain a look. Derain's grunt was inaudible as he moved toward the last interloper and knocked his boots free of the hull.

The lock opened with a slight hiss and ice fragments pelted Luli's suit. Everyone sidled up against the walls as she shut the outer door. Their comm channel cleared of the static as the hull of the ship blocked the confounder's signal. "So far so good, no sensors tripped," Luli whispered to the group. "Now for the inner door."

The lock filled with air as Derain stared into the ship from the inner window. No warning lights and no guards wandered by. "Never trust in luck", he muttered under his breath. The chamber pressurized and the inner hatch opened. Luli dropped the bag she had been carrying into a corner.

Jacquie and Barney headed down the port passage as Derain led Luli to a data port. She jacked in and started running through the rosters.

"This is a pretty big vessel. Multiple levels, but it was powered down for sleep travel." She glanced at the low lighting and continued, "Not many active life forms on board, so low heat and low oxy levels running throughout the ship. Your fugitive is pretty close to where they currently have Rabbit stashed, but he is up and about." She looked quizzically at Derain, "Is he part of the crew?"

Derain shrugged in return. She unplugged herself from the port, "Looks like we're following the Captain." She keyed her group channel, "Captain, we're en route to you. Looks like both targets are on the third deck, in the aft compartments."

Creaks and groans emanated from the walls as they moved forward, checking each hallway they passed for any of the ship's crew. They eventually caught up with Jacquie and Barney at a lift. They went down to the third deck as a group.

"We didn't come across anyone, did you?" asked Luli.

"Not a soul," replied the Captain. "Almost seems too quiet for a prison transport." She glanced at each of them in turn. "Keep your wits about you... something's giving me the wigglies."

Barney took point and Derain drifted back to the rear. The engineer sidled back to them and gave the 'all clear'. They kept their eyes peeled as they continued to move toward the aft section. With the ship's interior lights being mostly dark and a thin layer of frost on the walls, the ship carried a feeling of abandonment.

"Luli, how many were registered as crew on the manifest?" Jacquie asked in low tones.

"Crew is fifteen with another ten listed as guards. Total lives on board are two hundred eighty seven. There was another entry for one more, but it wasn't listed as human. Wonder what it is?" Luli checked her internal guide, "We're almost there. It should be the next one down."

Derain slid to the left of the hatch, pistol drawn as Barney went to a knee just to the right. Luli kept watch down the hallway as Jacquie reached for the handle. As she slowly unlatched it, Barney sighted down his barrel through the crack. The lights were dim, but there were only seated prisoners to be seen.

"Clear," Barney said as he edged into the room. Jacquie followed him in, while Derain and

Luli took up positions outside the door. Barney kept pace with Jacquie as she moved on down the line of seated, sleeping prisoners. She stopped once she came up to Rabbit. His wiry body slumped against the wall and stubble dotted his long, olive skinned face. He looked much older than she remembered; more worn, almost lean. She shook him lightly as she placed her hand over his mouth. "Anton... Anton, wake up."

Out in the hallway, Derain asked Luli, "How close is the skip right now? The sooner we collect him, the sooner we can get out of here."

"He hasn't moved much since we boarded. Just a few rooms down and to the left." She keyed the group comm, "Captain, all good on your front? We're ready to bag the next target."

"Aye, we have him. We'll be heading out soon," replied Barney. He looked at Jacquie as Anton's blue eyes fluttered open. The look of concern on her face disappeared as Rabbit's eyes spied her. He was startled upon seeing who it was, but made no sound, seeing the finger raised to Jacquie's lips. She pulled her hand away from his mouth and stepped back. The sharp sound of grinding metal rung out as Barney pried the steel restraints off his wrists then cut the straps holding him down. Anton got up slowly. He staggered as he stretched his legs and back.

He looked back and forth down the line of prisoners and made a plaintive face at Jacquie. Barney harrumphed and started cutting all the straps holding the prisoners down while Jacquie looked for the wrist lock controls. With a loud click all of the restraints opened. Anton raised his finger to his lips and Jacquie gave him a disbelieving glare. Barney chuckled lightly as they all left the room.

"Leave it open. Give them a chance to get out of there," Anton said as he rubbed his wrists. "Where's Luli? You guys are still traveling together, right?"

***

Luli and Derain came to the hatch that blinked on Luli's HUD.

"This is the one," she said. "You ready?"

Derain nodded and pulled out his Bounty Hunter ID to make sure it was easily viewable.

Pistols drawn, the two of them opened the hatch and stepped into what could only be described as a bloodbath. The white plas-tile walls were splashed red with blood and the floor drain was full to overflowing. There were a few badly beaten bodies thrown into a corner of the room while an unnaturally pale woman hung from chains bolted to the wall across from the hatch. A stocky man in a blood splashed lab coat stood in front of the woman with a scalpel in hand. The two other men in the room turned at the opening of the hatch.

Jon Gray Lang

Derain shouted, "Official bounty business!"

They both went for their weapons as Luli and Derain each fired. Their shots rang out loudly in the enclosed room and both men went down. The man in the lab coat slowly turned toward them as Derain knocked the scalpel from his hand. Luli kept them covered while Derain wrestled with the man until he had him subdued.

The man kept babbling the entire time, "It's in her head. It's in her head! Sensors have been going crazy and all this time it's been in her head." He started giggling.

Derain tied the man's wrists together and then pulled out his data pad. He compared the face on the screen with the man's face. He nodded in approval, "Glad to see my contact is still good on his word. Hello Doctor Saric. Well, pretending to be a doctor these days, aren't you?" He lifted the fugitive up as the woman on the wall began to shudder.

"I'm cutting her down," Luli stated. She holstered her pistol as she walked forward to slip the bonds that held the lady in place.

The youngish looking woman slumped forward as her bonds to the wall were released. Her short dark hair was matted with blood and Luli could see skull through the flaps of skin. "Looks like your doctor friend was slicing into her head for some reason. She's been pretty heavily beaten, too. What a mess." Luli could see the remnants of old bruises underneath the newer ones. She carried her over to a less begrimed spot on the floor and gave her the once over. She might have a broken rib and it looked like her wrist was sprained. Considering how old some of these bruises were, she was in better condition than Luli initially had expected.

"Why are you messing with that thing?" Derain demanded. "It's just a genorg; a drone."

Just then, the Captain, Barney and Anton stepped into the room. "Hey Luli, it's good to see you again," said Anton as he walked over to give her a hug.

"It's good to see you too, Anton." She hugged him back.

No one saw the genorg stand up. It moved jerkily toward the Doctor like a marionette with some missing strings. Its left foot suddenly kicked out and the crunching sound of the Doctor's windpipe echoed in the small room. Everyone stared in shock as the drone fell to the deck as if its puppeteer had suddenly cut the remaining strings. The Doctor slowly choked to death on his own blood in the silent room. Derain backed up, kicked the woman in the side and swore, "He was worth more alive! That's half the value on him now. Fucking drone!" he cursed as he kicked her again.

"That's not just any drone, by the way. That, my friends," stated Anton Roane, as he gestured at the woman on the floor, "is the Butcher of Timmony Bay."

three

The Dead Horse Shanty

"This thing is the Butcher of Timmony Bay?" queried Jacquie.

"She sure is," claimed Anton.

"Damn it! I still can't believe it killed him. He's almost not worth the trouble now," cursed Derain Tiwi. He mumbled under his breath, "Now I have to drag his carcass all the way back to the ship. I swear this job isn't worth it sometimes." He kicked the woman on the ground one more time as he bent over to throw the doctor's body over his shoulder. "Well, we've got everyone we came to get. The sooner we're out of here, the happier I'll be."

Everyone started to leave the room except Anton, "She's coming with us."

The Captain turned around and said quietly, "That thing is not getting on board my ship.

Jon Gray Lang

From what I've just seen, it is too unpredictable. From the moniker you just gave it; it is too dangerous."

"Never mind that it gives me the creeps." Derain shifted the dead weight of the Doctor on his shoulder, "This guy is heavier than I expected. He's not much bigger than Barney. What's he been eating?"

Anton stood his ground, "I'm sorry Jacq, but I won't go without her." He slowly bent over to pick her up. She seemed so much smaller than he remembered. He threw her lightly over his shoulder and headed for the hatch and back out to the hall.

"We'll straighten this out on Matilda," Jacquie promised. "Let's go."

Barney once again took point as they all headed back toward the airlock. He stopped and waved everyone back. The outcry of people shouting and what sounded like fighting echoed from up ahead. He slowly made his way down the hall and came across a large group of prisoners scuffling with some of the crew. A crewman started firing blindly into the crowd and backpedaling as fast he could. The other crewmen followed him. With a roar, the prisoners gave chase. Barney waited to make sure all was clear before he waved everyone forward.

He spied the same group of crewmen further along as they ran toward an escape pod. More shots were fired as they pulled open the hatch and stumbled into the pod. The prisoners ran for the hatch and were pulling at it to pry it open. The ship's alarm started to wail and the decks glowed in the sudden red light.

Luli turned to Anton, "Your friends work quickly, Rabbit. Are they releasing everybody?"

"They're not my friends. I just repaid a debt."

The team picked up their pace as they headed back to the airlock. With the alarm blaring, there was no longer any need for secrecy. Altercations between more groups of prisoners and crew became commonplace as their screams and yells echoed all through the Vogelgesang.

"Do you have a plan for getting us back, Jacq? I'm not exactly dressed for a spacewalk, nor is she." Anton pointed to his burden.

"Shut your mouth. We've got it covered for two more. Are you really trying to push me right now?" Jacquie grittily replied.

Luli gave Anton a look to keep quiet as did Barney. They had been lucky so far. Roving gangs of escapees were running all over the prison vessel without rhyme or reason. "The airlock should be right around the next corner," Luli stated into the group comm. As they neared their airlock, they came across a very large group of prisoners who seemed to be headed to the bridge of the ship.

"Rabbit! That you?" one of them called out. "Are you who got us free?" asked another.

"Yeah, it's me, Sam. Hey, Rosa. It looks like some old friends just couldn't continue to live without the glorious me," he smiled as he indicated the small group. Jacquie rolled her eyes. The ship shuddered as a life boat launched. "Shouldn't be much more crew left on board. You should be able to take the bridge pretty easily."

"That's the plan, of course. Old Jimmy here says he can fly this crate. What you got over your shoulder? That her?" replied Sam.

"It is, yeah. I have special plans for her, Sam. Special plans," said Anton.

"Glad to hear it. You lost more than most of us because of that creature." Sam squinted strangely at him, "Always coming through in the pinch, aren't you. You have a strange luck, Rabbit, but I'm willing to use it one more time. Maybe we'll cross paths again." He shook hands with Anton before the gang of prisoners headed on their way.

"Any time would be too soon, Sam," Anton whispered, wiping his hand against his pant leg. The ship shuddered as another life boat launched.

Chaos seemed to hold sway as they came across pockets of prisoners who fought amongst themselves; old rivalries were no longer held in check by the guards.

"We need to hurry up or we're not getting off this boat," Derain declared. They hurried around the last corner to see the airlock before them.

Jon Gray Lang

Luli cycled the first door and everyone piled in after her. She turned to the crew, "Suits are in the bag, Anton. Get her and yourself suited up as fast as you can. Captain, watch the hatch for intruders! This'll be a short trip to nowhere if they realize we have a way out. We need to blow this boat and get back home." She checked her own suit and locked her helmet back in place. Jacquie and Barney locked their helmets while Derain tied the body of the doctor to his suit in preparation. Barney helped Anton get the woman into the spare suit and Luli tied her to Anton after he was completely suited up.

"Everyone ready?" Luli asked as the ship shuddered again. "Sounds like the last of the crew got off this vessel. Now it's our turn. Here we go!"

She cycled in the outer door and the whoosh of the last bits of the atmosphere blew out into space. They all linked to one another. Luli fired her hip jets and like a ribbon, they floated out into space; back toward Matilda.

"It'll be good to see home again," Anton whispered.

Though she was dark and hard to see in the blackness of space, Luli could feel her floating there, like a beacon of hope. Matilda's battered hull blocked out more of the stars as she grew closer. A few touches on her attitudinal jets and Luli reached for the grips off the flight deck. The others scrabbled for a hold and their forward travel came to a slow halt. One by one, they each pulled the next one toward the hangar doors. Once everyone was in, Derain hit the controls that would close the doors.

"Goodbye Vogelgesang. I hardly knew ya," muttered Anton as the hangar doors clanged shut. He eyed the small craft sitting in the hangar and turned to Derain, "That your bird, mister? She looks pretty tough."

Derain just growled as he strapped the dead body to the wall and followed the others to the airlock.

four

Spanish Ladies

As they changed out of their suits, Jacquie swung her helmet up against Anton's head and knocked him back into the wall. She strode over to him, grabbed a handful of his suit and warned, "Do not ever question my authority on my ship or what comes aboard my ship. Do you hear me?" She waited a brief moment, before she continued, "I said, do you hear and understand me?"

Anton blearily nodded at her. She let go of him and he slid to the deck. "Derain. Barney. Take that to lockdown now," she ordered as she pointed at the genorg. "Luli, get us the hell out of here ASAP. We need to vacate this block of space. We've already been here too long."

Everyone quick stepped out of there as soon as they could, leaving Anton and the Captain alone in the airlock changing room.

Anton looked up at her while trying to staunch the flow of blood from his nose, "I thindk you brodke my nobse."

"It's not all I'm going to break if you don't listen to me and do as I say," she said as she handed him a med pack. She murmured as she continued, "You know I love you and I don't want to hurt you, but if any decision you make harms any of my people, I will." She looked away as he blotted at the blood coming from his nose, "Anyway, it's good to have you back on board." She looked back at him, "Do you think you'll be staying with us long?"

Anton shifted as he continued to change out of his borrowed suit. With a few snorts, the blood stopped flowing and his breathing cleared. "Since it doesn't appear that you did, in fact, break my nose and I have absolutely nowhere else to go and I owe you everything... Well, to put it more simply, I don't have any current plans, at all, so to speak. I was hoping to make a less bloody appearance, but I guess the precedence for that was set a long time ago." He stood up and saluted, "So, Captain Jacquotte Delahaye, may I come aboard? At least until we make planet fall?"

The ship lurched as it got under way and Anton fell against Jacquie as she replied, "Always Anton, always."

***

Jon Gray Lang

Barney and Derain carried the woman down to where the bounty hunter cages that they used for lockdown were located. "Why was your skip cutting into her head, you think?" Barney asked. "Might be a good idea to get her down to sickbay and check her out." He gave the woman a once over, "She's in pretty bad shape, too. Pretty sure the Captain isn't going to want her to die out here."

"Who cares if it dies, it's already cost me a lot of money," replied Derain. "And it's not a 'her'; it's a drone, a genorg. Don't forget that Barney." Derain continued to think out loud, "Though it does have a known history. Hmm, might actually be worth something."

Barney rolled his eyes. "I think we should get 'it' to sickbay then. We already have one dead body on board, and I, for one, don't want to make it two," Barney retorted.

"While it's getting scanned, we'll have to lock it down," muttered Derain. "One of the older med tubes should work. I don't think it will be getting up anytime soon."

The two of them brought the woman down to the sickbay, stripped her and placed her in one of the med tubes. Derain reached in and pulled a pair of dog tags from around her neck before he locked it shut, "I think I'll keep these for now."

Barney set the scanners and turned to the mechanical doctor, "Scan this living genetically modified organism and see what we can do to keep her from dying. You got that?"

"Eee chu tae dom sah," replied the robot doctor.

"Just do it. Always wants to fight that thing does," muttered Barney.

"You've got this Barney? I need to talk with the contractee and see what I can get for our recently acquired property," Derain said as he left the sickbay.

"Swear that man has a one track mind sometimes." Barney asked the med bot, "Are you scanning her yet?"

"Che dom sae to," it replied.

Barney shouted as he walked out of sickbay, "Keep me informed then, got it? I'll let the others know." He keyed the ship's comm pad right outside the hatch, "Bridge, our, uh, guest is locked in a med tube. I've got Doc running a scan to see how bad off she is."

He wandered up to the lift and exited on to the second deck. He cut through the gym as he continued toward his domain. Once he was in the main shaft, he free floated down toward the engine room and the throbbing weirdness that was the jump engine. An oppressive feeling encircled him as he stepped through the hatch and the heavy gravity brought his feet to the deck. A sigh escaped him as the impression that he was no longer alone settled around him. Someone or something else felt trapped in there with him. This feeling had grown more so of late. He screwed up his face and walked over to his work station and began to run tests on the device.

"I will figure you out, thing. I will. Once I do, I'll know where it is we go when you jump. I promise." He placed his headphones on to block out everything else from his pet project.

***

Luli already had the ship under way to Chalman's world as the Captain wandered onto the bridge. "I want to offload our cargo as soon as possible, Lu. We're already behind with this side jaunt and I'd like to make up as much time as possible. And before you say it, without the use of 'that' machine. We need to have the gate registry in this system; otherwise there'll be hell to pay."

"Already en route, Captain. Never doubt your pilot, its bad luck." Luli smiled at her.

"You and your patois. Once we are locked in, come on down to the lounge to celebrate. The job went well, a pretty clean run. Can't really ask for more."

"Yes sir, Captain, sir." Luli threw a sloppy salute to the Captain's back as she exited the bridge. She bent over and picked up her ukulele and strummed as she sang, "Farewell and adieu, to ye fair Spanish Ladies, farewell and adieu ye ladies of Spain..."

five

Whiskey in the Jar

Luli quietly strummed her ukulele in the corner of the lounge while Derain plugged away at his data pad. Anton and Barney shared some anecdote that caused Barney to chuckle long enough to forget where he was in his game of solitaire. It was at this point that Jacquie walked in. She lifted her hand which clutched a bottle that contained a brownish liquid as she called out, "I'm pulling out a bottle of our best for a job well done, everyone. Though, truth be told, this is a bottle of our only."

There were a few dry laughs around as she collected a handful of tumblers and brought them over to the big table. Everyone put down what they had been doing and got up to wander over to the table. The Captain poured five glasses to the top.

She lifted her glass and everyone lifted theirs in response. "Salud!" she shouted as she threw back the drink.

Everyone chimed in with a salute and the clatter of the glasses impacting on the table echoed in the room.

Anton sputtered and coughed, "Either I don't know the good stuff anymore or times are a lot harder than I remember."

"Well, she did say this was the only bottle on board," Luli snickered.

Anton grimaced before he gave a small bow, "Jacquie, thanks for rescuing this humble man once again."

"Humble my ass," piped up Barney.

"And it's good to see the infamous Barnabus de Lagnel again!" Anton replied as he glanced in engineer's direction. "I am ever so glad to see you're still traveling with these two, Luli."

"He asked about you, he did," Barney interjected.

"This gentleman here, I do not know," Anton pointed at Derain. "I would like to thank you as well. My name is Anton Roane."

"The Great and Glorious, he'll have you believe," Barney continued.

Anton pointedly ignored Barney, "And you are?"

"That is Derain Tiwi, our bounty hunter at large. Hunting fugitives and other lowlifes throughout the known systems," Luli said with mock emphasis. "And it's good to see you alive too, Anton."

"I've heard about you," deadpanned Derain as he returned to his data pad. "To change the topic, I have garnered a new deal for our dear, dead, Doctor."

"Dear to you maybe," Barney muttered into his empty glass.

Derain continued over Barney, "The loss won't be quite as big as I had originally thought and I don't even have to go that far to collect it. Just a short jaunt to Caleb's moon. Seems his head is wanted almost as much as the rest of him. I might even be able to afford a replacement for that bottle." He winked at Jacquie.

"Good to hear that, Derain. We should be able to drop your ship at Caleb's before dropping cargo at Chalman's," said the Captain as she rolled the now empty glass back and forth between her hands. "Which brings us to the next point. What exactly do we have on board in sickbay right now? How concerned should we be?"

Barney spoke up, "Doc got back to me regarding our, uh, guest. It looks like she isn't going to die from her wounds any time soon. The cuts to her head are superficial; she has a broken rib and ankle. Doc did mention that an anomaly cropped up. There is some sort of electronic apparatus lodged in her skull. Doc isn't really sure what it's for or how long it's been there. I scanned it for any outgoing signals, but it's clear."

Jon Gray Lang

Luli piped up, "I remember the skip babbling about something being in her head. Now that I think about it, all those bodies in the corner had had their scalps cut through, also."

"She's heavily sedated right now, but we made sure to put her in lock down. She won't be going anywhere, anytime soon," continued Barney. "I have Doc keeping an eye on her, too."

"Thank you Barney," replied the Captain. "That drone is a strange one. Something about it is different, off seeming. We'll keep her on ice until we figure out what to do with her."

Derain looked up at Jacquie at this point. She gave him a nod. He threw her the dog tags as he explained, "This is what I've been able to find out so far. First off, those tags are real. Your friend Anton here is right."

Never doubt the Rabbit," Anton intoned.

Derain pointedly continued, "It does seem to be the drone known as the Butcher of Timmony Bay. It is, or was anyway, a standard drone model. Someone went to the trouble to give it the name Galena Chadov." He wondered out loud, "I can't imagine why would someone bother naming a genorg? It's not like it's a person. Where was I? He perused his data pad, "Oh yes, she ended up ranking as a Lieutenant during the police action on Tigron. That part of the case always stuck out to me. How did a drone become an officer? Anyway, her platoon was one of the few Consortium forces to survive the first few waves until extraction. She was awarded a citation for keeping her platoon alive, as well as, other members of the Consortium. That is, until the truth of her actions on Tigron came to light."

"What was it? Thirty counts of murder were levied against her and then she was blamed for the food distribution fiasco after they dropped a nuke on Tigron?" Luli stated. "Always sounded like they needed a scapegoat to pin the ugliness of that military disaster on."

Jacquie gazed at Anton, "That's when we lost track of you, Anton. Isn't that when you were captured and tried as a terrorist?"

His eyes got dark for a moment, "Yes. Her team had captured our position even though we outnumbered them. It was late in the fight when food and resources were light. She had us line up and kneel as she walked behind us and shot us one by one in the back of the head. She did leave a few of us alive, like me, and kept us as prisoners." He fiddled with his hands, "We were tried and locked up in that kangaroo of a court. We barely received any news during our incarceration. But even we heard about her trial."

"The last entry I was able to find was that she was court-martialed after her platoon testified against her. Then she simply disappeared," Derain finished.

"I remember that. She was being shipped out for a public execution and her transport never arrived," said Luli. "How did she end up out here?"

Anton replied, "I don't know. I recognized her at detainment, but she wasn't housed with the rest of us." He looked around, "I know she's a drone and they're all supposed to be the same, but she isn't like the other ones. Maybe they did something to her; maybe she was just made different. It's just... I can't forget that day. I won't ever forget those eyes... filled with a sense of purpose... and with loss. She seemed to recognize me at the loading dock too. I, I don't know anything more."

"We'll have to figure out what to do with her soon. See what else you can find, Derain." She turned toward Anton, "Lastly, Anton, are you going to stay with us past Chalman's?"

He shrugged his shoulders as he gazed at Jacquie with a slightly questioning look, "I'd like to stay if you'll have me. It was a bad three years on that rock. I could use some freedom and I could use some peace." He mustered his thoughts before he continued, "You already know I'm a wanted man. Your bounty hunter friend should be able to prove that with ease. Never mind you just broke me out of a prison ship. You may want to take that into account before you decide to have me stay on board."

"Anton, you know you'll always have a place on my ship. We'll deal with anything that comes our way as a team... as family." Jacquie made eye contact for a moment, "I have your back. Hopefully you still have mine too."

"That counts for me too," declared Luli.

Barney uttered with a light smile, "I still love you, lad. Would be nice to have you back on board a while. Things have been almost quiet since you left."

Anton looked toward Derain who simply stipulated, "Her ship; her rules. What she says goes." Derain stood and offered his hand to Anton. After they shook he continued, "I'm still going to keep my eye on you. I don't know you. We don't have history. I have absolutely no qualms about putting you down." He slid back into the chair.

Anton concluded the conversation with, "It's good to know where I stand with everyone." He stared directly at Derain, "The warning is taken."

six

Born Under a Bad Sign

Galena woke up surrounded by darkness. She slowly reached around and felt curved walls very close to her head and sides. There was another one next to her feet. Was she in some sort of coffin?

She started to hyperventilate until she spied some indistinct lights blinking to the left of her. This small glimmer of technology allowed her to calm down. She felt along her sides and came to the realization that she was naked and in a med tube. More information that meant she was still alive. How damaged was she though? To be stored in a med tube usually meant a bad injury. She ran her hand along her torso and discovered an adheso-band stretched taut across her abdomen.

Slowly poking and prodding, she

Jon Gray Lang

grunted as she came across a rib, "A broken rib, Okay. So far, not too bad. Left wrist is aching, possibly sprained." She applied pressure with her fingertips around her head and felt queasy when she pressed on her short cropped, blood matted hair. She worked slowly around her scalp and came across multiple plasflesh patches. A small cry escaped her lips when she pushed a little too hard on the largest of these patches.

All of a sudden, she heard a trundling noise and saw the indistinct lights headed toward her. She dropped her hands to her chest and closed her eyes as the machine came to a stop beside the med tube. It made querying noises as it touched what she assumed was the interface built into the surface of the med tube. She slowed her breathing.

"It's just a med bot, nothing to be concerned with." She heard it slowly trundle away. The tightness in her chest eased just as she noticed that her tags were missing.

"Where are they?" In a panic, she searched her body for any sign of them; then felt along the sides of the med tube. She became more frantic at their loss. She started hyperventilating again and had to pause to get her breathing under control. "Must... relax... can't set off the med sensor." It took a moment but she finally got her breathing under control. Questions rose to her mind, "I have no idea where I am or who has me or why?"

She felt along the med tube until she

found the latch. It appeared to be locked from the outside. This med tube was old military hardware from what she could tell. If she remembered correctly, one had to jimmy the latch just right to have it pop. She felt the latch give and felt the slight decompression of the chamber. She breathed a sigh of relief as she lifted the lid just enough to squeeze out and land on her toes. She squatted down, closed the lid and scanned the room.

This was a med lab on what looked to be a military craft variant, but not one that was familiar to her. A med bot model she didn't recognize hung from the ceiling. It held its multiple arms close to its torso as it did whatever med bots do. Luckily, it hadn't noticed her as of yet, but it would once the med tube registered that it was no longer being occupied. At that moment the med bot stirred and swung toward the med tube she was hidden behind.

Fight or flight instantly kicked in and she ran toward the med bot; jumped onto a stack of crates and landed halfway up its torso. She grabbed hand holds that she used to climb the automaton. It bleated as it grabbed for her with its many arms, but adrenaline fueled her and it missed. Galena started to pull out all the cables that connected it to the ceiling. The machine's bleats and whirs grew louder as she kept pulling cables until the lights went dim. She let go and fell. Her ankle gave on landing and her head smacked against the decking.

She lay on the floor, stunned, "Bad

idea. Not really in the right shape to do this." She waited for the dizziness to pass. "What to do, what to do. Get my tags back then get off this ship."

She looked around and spied her clothes piled in a corner, still stiff with her blood. After putting them on, she rifled through the drawers until she came across a scalpel. She palmed it and keyed the hatch.

She found herself in a large cargo bay with huge holding tanks to the port side and a land vehicle up ahead and to starboard. The room was cold enough that she could see her breath. She gave an involuntary shiver. Variously sized cargo containers were stacked neatly and tied down to the deck grating. She spied a lift tube that was partially hidden far to the left as she moved toward the tanks. She keyed the lift to come down and hid in case someone was on board. The lift came down without incident.

There were four decks on this craft. She pondered quietly, "The Bridge would be on the top deck; not sure I want to go there. Living space should be on the deck below that." She muttered out loud, "That's if this old crate is built like most ships." She pushed the lift button for the third deck and sidled up against the left wall.

The door opened as the lift stopped on the third deck. She noticed that there was a quick bend to the right. She crept up to the corner and peered down the long hallway at a series of hatches on both sides. The first hatch on the left had more separation from the next set of hatches than the others. Aside from that one, they all seemed equally spaced. She noticed height marks scratched into the corner with various ages listed. The name Jacquotte was written as if by a child near these marks. She muttered to herself, "The biggest one. Might as well start with it then."

Galena stepped up to the hatch and listened, but no sound seemed to emanate through the hatch. She sucked in a steadying breath and changed her grip on the scalpel. She quietly opened the hatch plate and snuck in.

There was a single low light on the short desk in the small room. It gave just enough light for her to see by. Galena could barely make out a woman on the only bed in the cabin. The woman's dark, straight hair spilled over the pillow, but there was no movement besides the slow and steady breath of sleep. A small glint caught the corner of her eye. Her dog tags were draped over a small ceramic cup that sat on the desk. Galena's breathing accelerated slightly as she grabbed the tags and put them around her neck. She held them in her hand when she heard an indrawn breath behind her.

***

On the bridge, Luli kept a slow monitor on their planned arrival time to Caleb's Moon when the silent alarm went off in sickbay. She pulled the current activity report from the lab and it revealed that one of the med tubes had recently been vacated. She tried to chime Doc, but there was no response. The lift now listed as sitting at Deck 3. She keyed the lounge comm, "Derain, you there?"

Derain glanced at the comm pad. He walked over to it and keyed the open channel back, "I'm here. What's up Lu?"

"Looks like our guest may be on the move on the third deck. Would you care to take a look?"

"On my way. Derain out."

Anton walked over to the comm and keyed back to the bridge, "We're both on our way, Luli. Keep an eye out, will you?"

"Already got the bridge in lockdown," she replied.

Derain gave him a look as he laid his data pad down and checked his pistol. Both men headed for the lift. As the door to the lift opened on the third deck, Derain drew his pistol. Anton stepped ahead of him toward the right bend in the short hall. The lift shifted behind them as it went down. Anton made head motions to Derain and pointed at the Captain's cabin. Derain rolled his eyes and waved him forward. They both took up positions to the sides of the hatch. The two of them did a silent countdown, then Anton swung it open. With the hatch open, they burst in to find Galena crouched over Jacquie with a scalpel pressed against her neck. A glint from the tags winked in the dark as they both stepped into the room.

"Get this bitch off me," grated Jacquotte Delahaye.

Galena pressed the scalpel against Jacquie's throat as she looked directly at Derain, "You will get me off this boat or she dies."

Anton slowly moved forward as he said, "You don't want to do this Galena. She's here to help you, to help us. She got both of us off that ship." He reached his hand forward, indicating the scalpel, "Why don't you give me that?" Galena looked confused for a moment, "Rabbit? What are you doing here?"

Jacquie struck at this very moment, knocking her elbow into Galena's chin. The scalpel clattered to the decking as her eyes rolled up into her head. Her body slumped over Jacquie's.

Jacquie spat quite vehemently as she pushed the genorg off of her bed, "This thing is not staying on board my ship."

seven

Nobody's Fault but Mine

Anton checked all the bandages along Galena's frame, but they still seemed to be in decent shape. She looked so small in her bloody pants and shirt. Her pale skin, which marked her as a genorg, shown through her short cropped dark hair. It reflected in the light as he and Barney carried her back to the lift. He stared at her face, waiting for those green eyes to open, but there was nothing, not even the flutter of an eyelid. They stepped off the lift onto the second deck and headed down to the machine room. Once inside, Barney opened one of Derain's containment cages that he used for his living bounties. Anton placed her inside and stepped back. Barney made doubly sure that the cage was locked tight.

"I'm going down to sickbay to see if

she broke anything," Barney proclaimed as he headed back to the hatch of the gym. "Luli said she couldn't reach Doc earlier."

"I'll be heading back in a moment." Anton continued to stare at Galena as he muttered, "How did we end up on the same prison transport, Lieutenant Galena Chadov? Chance? Planned?" He moved away from the cage and shut the hatch to the machine room. "Might as well work some of this stress out," he said as he made his way toward the weight system in the gym.

Over the ship's comm, Barney's voice rang out, "She's torn out all of Doc's controllers! This is going take a few days to repair!" The vexation in his voice rang out loudly, "How long till we reach Chalman's?"

Luli's voice announced, "Four solar days, Barney. You need help down there?"

There was a long pause before Barney's growl came through loud and clear, "I need a tall person!"

Anton chuckled to himself as he started doing reps. Space travel could weaken you faster than anything. Even with the artificial gravity built into most ships, it was still something you had to work at to keep it from debilitating you. It didn't help that he'd been aboard a prison ship in sleep mode for however long. It was a common tactic to keep new prisoners weak once they got to their shiny new prison planet. It made troublemakers easier to beat into shape and less work to control.

"Somehow Jacq saved my ass again," he said out loud. He stopped lifting for a moment to stroke the wall of the ship, "It's good to be back on board you, Matilda. Really good." His hand slid down the wall to hang loosely at his side, "You have no idea how good."

***

Luli could hear Barney's curses from the cargo bay as she walked toward the med lab. The hatch was already open, tools were strewn all about, and Barney was splicing a cable attached to Doc.

"At least he's still coupled to the ceiling," she said as she stepped in. "She really did a number, huh? What can I help you with first?"

"I'll give her this; it's actually not as bad as it looks. She pulled all the cables. And I mean all of them. Some separated cleanly, others, eh, not so much," Barney indicated the cable in his lap. "The hard part, for me... is she pulled them all out from the ceiling instead of from his chassis. So I need a tall person, you since you showed up, to climb up there and check the ports for damage." He went back to splicing the damaged cable. "Oh and cross your fingers or whatever that luck thing you do is."

Luli peered at him before she walked over to stare up Doc's chassis.

"Don't give me that 'oh-I'm-too-old-

and-feeble to climb the robot' line. If I look half as good as you do at your age, I'll be amazed. Now get your ancient ass up there. I have a strange feeling we might need Doc very soon," Barney said as he gave her a glare.

Luli laughed as she nimbly climbed the robot and angled herself for a solid perch to check the sixteen ports. The first few had detached cleanly, but the fifth one still had a broken line clinging to it. She pried it loose with a small knife that she always carried. The broken cable clattered to the deck as she moved onto the next one. She started prying another broken cable piece loose when she asked, "Barney, does Anton seem unusual to you? More distant than the last time we saw him?"

"He just seems lost to me. As if he isn't quite sure he's still the Rabbit." He looked up at her, "You've got to keep in mind he's been through quite a lot since the last time he was onboard."

Another piece of cabling fell to the deck with a clatter as she replied, "I realize that. He just seems so different. Almost like the man I knew, but like a part of him has gone missing." She grunted for a moment as another broken cable chunk fell. "Just a couple more. Most of these separated like they're supposed to." She changed her angle to pry at a broken hydraulic cable. "Maybe that's all it is then. Maybe he's trying to figure out who he is now. Ugh, this hydraulic line is a mess.

I'm going to need a rag to even see how bad this one is."

Barney reached into a pocket and threw a balled up rag to her. She caught it and wiped down the connection port. She wrapped the rag around the line and gave it a twist as she pulled. It separated with a wet sucking sound. Hydraulic fluid drained onto the decking, just narrowly missing Luli.

"Ha! Almost got me," she crowed in elation. "Working on the last one now. Do you think we'll ever get the same Rabbit back?"

Barney stopped what he was doing and contemplated her question, "Are you the same person you were after your last journey from the Sol system? The last time you saw home?"

"Good point." The last broken connector fell. "Not to change topics, but I will, what do you think we're going to do with our rather troublesome guest? Captain is pretty pissed."

Barney grouched, "I'm pretty pissed myself. She's here less than a solar day and holds Jacquie at knife point. Never mind what she did to Doc. Definitely not happy with our guest either." He slowly screwed the threading plate back over the end of the cable he was working on. "Once you get this one in, we should be able to, in theory, get Doc back on line." He passed the cable up to Luli as he continued, "She has to go. Where or how, not up to me, but she has to go."

She angled to the main port and

screwed it in tight.   "She's a lot more trouble than one would expect, I agree. Aah, there we go."

Doc started lighting up as a deep hum filled the room. The med bot stuttered in place and almost knocked Luli off. "Eee tu cha dae son ta. Eee tu cha dae son ta!"

"Doc, calm down.   Calm down!" Barney shouted as he stood up, brushing off his knees. "Run a diagnostic."

"Che du tong sa," replied the med bot.

"We're working on it. Relax. Over excitable machine," spouted Barney as Luli laughed in the background. "Luli, I'm going to pass you the other good cables and lines. We'll see how bad off we are in the short run."   He walked around collecting the good cables and passed them up to her.   "So, one broken hydraulic line and three damaged cables."

Doc started waving three of its arms around, "Sa tad don da!"

"I just said that!" yelled Barney. "Cranky robot. I'll get you fixed when I get you fixed! Now, finish up that diagnostic and let me know what else is broken in you, you mechanical moaner."

Luli leapt to the decking and wiped her hands on the dirty rag. "Let me know when you need those reconnected, Okay Barney? I'm going to head back up topside to see how we're doing on time."

***

Derain stopped just inside the bridge to cycle the hatch closed. The Captain was seated at the weapons station, pouring over the screen. He stood still for a moment just to watch her as she leaned back to stretch and released a pent up breath.

"That you, Derain? Had a feeling you'd come up here to go over your drop off." She spun the chair to face him and raised her fingers to her temples, "I sense this is one of those under the table deals."

Derain replied as he took the seat at the navigation station, "Actually it should go pretty smoothly. Not that I trust the bastards, but it should be fine. What I really wanted to discuss is what we're going to do with the genorg, Galena Chadov."

"Space it or leave it on Chalman's World. I am up for spacing it. Pretty sure the rest of them would rather drop it off, though." She gave him a questioning look, "Why? Do you have a better idea?"

He got a sly look in his eyes, "I just so happen to know that there is an active bounty on her, and it's on Chalman's. My thought is we drop the cargo on time, drop the drone for a few extra mazuma and then move on to our next job. The hardest part will be convincing the rest of the crew."

Jacquie shrugged, "Easy enough. At least you found a plan that might pay off. We're getting pretty low on foodstuffs and this extra jaunt to Caleb is going to stretch our water reserves. We'll already need to hold over on Chalman's longer than I would like. Maybe Luli can play a few shows to earn some dirt side currency," she pondered.

Derain questioned, "Any takers for hauling cargo off that rock? It helps me to know what bounties to look for if I know where we'll be heading next.

She replied, "Nothing yet. Still looking for one that pays well and won't be another long haul. This one is already taking longer than I wanted it to."

"Well, if you get any bites, you let me know as soon as you can. Mind if I take Luli for the drop?" he inquired.

She waved the question away, "If she's fine with it; I'm fine with it. Might as well get the future of our unwanted guest out of the way as soon as possible." She stood slowly and walked over to the ship's comm and keyed it on, "Luli, Barney, up to the bridge." She paused for a moment, "You too, Anton." She looked back at Derain and said, "Now we wait."

Anton was the last to enter the bridge. Barney sat on the weapons station with his legs dangling. Luli was in her pilot seat, but facing toward the Captain. The dangerous man whose name he couldn't quite remember was seated behind Jacquie at the navigation station. The bridge wasn't a big room and it felt crowded. He twisted the towel he had used to dry himself and placed it around his neck. With feigned calm, he leaned against the open wall next to the hatch.

The Captain stood in the middle of the bridge and waited until all eyes were on her, "Barney, where are we with Doc?"

"I should have him back up to full capacity in a couple of solar days," he replied. "My question is, what are we going to do with the one who broke Doc in the first place?"

"Funny you should ask, because that's what we're here to vote on." She looked around at her crew, "It is not staying on board my ship. There are two options on the table. We can space it now or we can turn it in for a bounty."

Luli looked as if she were about to say something when Anton interrupted her, "Space her? She's a living being, Jacq." He looked around at the others, "Has it gotten so hard out here that you would space a person without provocation?"

Derain barked a short laugh, "No provocation? It killed my bounty, wrecked Doc and then held the Captain at knife point. And it's not like it's a real person. It's just a drone; created from DNA slop to plow fields or dig mines or whatever other tasks those things are used for. It's just genorg trash."

"The way you bandy that word 'genorg' around Derain, it's beginning to sound pretty offensive to the only cyborg on this boat," Luli challenged.

"Luli, you were born. It's not the
same thing at all. That thing in the holding cage was
grown to be nothing more than a menial laborer,"
declared Derain. "Besides, this one is a wanted
murderer. You've seen what it can do. Do you want
to release it on some planet and see how much hell it
can raise?"

Barney interjected, "He's got a point,
Lu. She's made a mess of things here in less than a
day. What kind of havoc could she raise on a
planet? I'm for turning her in for the bounty."

Luli snarled, "Fine. Turn her over for
the bounty."

Anton glared at this group of people
that he thought of as his family. These same people
had just broken him out of a prison transport going
to who knows where and now they were voting on
whether to toss a woman out of the airlock. "I
won't have you space her, Jacq." He looked at
Derain, "Who wants her?"

"Local   security   officials.   No
Consortium thugs if that's what you're concerned
about," he assured.

Anton looked bitterly at the Captain,
"Last question I have. Why are you giving me a
vote, Jacq?"

She looked at him with a sad
kindness, "Because you're part of the crew and the
crew always gets to vote on the hard choices. You
know that."

"Still playing that card, are you? Fine

then, turn her in for the bounty." He turned toward the hatch, "If there isn't anything else, I feel the need to breathe some cleaner air." He stomped out the open hatch and made for the lift.

Barney got up and put his hand on the Captain's knee, "He'll understand. He's just going to need more time." He patted her knee and let his hand slide back down to his side, "I'm going to keep working on Doc. You mind coming down, Luli?"

"Right behind you," she declared. "I swear there used to be a time when we didn't have to make such dreadful choices."

"Are you sure? Seems like it's only been bad choices open to us for as long as I can remember," snapped Jacquie.

As she stepped through the hatch, Luli opined, "I've been around a lot longer than you. I swear the decisions weren't so awful sometime in the past half century."

After everyone else had left, Derain looked at the Captain and said, "That went pretty smoothly, wouldn't you say?"

eight

Keep on Moving

The Matilda was processed through the jump gate in the Aconda system to the one in the Rhada system without any trouble. The jump itself only took the standard solar hour of travel time. Over the next couple solar days, the ship stayed on track for Derain's rendezvous on Caleb's moon.

The Consortium wouldn't exist without the jump gates. Not only did the jump gates speed up travel between the systems for commerce, as most ships only had sublight engines, it also allowed a quick military response which included quarantines of entire systems.

Very few ships had any form of FTL capability. This was mainly due to the fact that the Consortium had made it illegal to own such a drive and the stipulation that they were costly to run. The military controlled the technology and only their larger capital ships had the capability. These drives required a massive amount of energy to generate a worm hole for the ship to travel through.

The jump gates worked under the same principle, but were 'fixed' at certain points in space which were on the outer edges of each system. These jump gate facilities were crewed by Consortium soldiers and this is how they kept a stranglehold on all travel. Merchants needed to show a registry for each jump gate it went through or their cargo was considered illegal contraband. The same was true for commuter craft. Control of the jump gates allowed the Consortium to track all commerce and the travel of any ship. The only legal option for those who wished not to be monitored was to take a sleeper ship journey, but these could take decades or longer to complete.

With the available time on board, before Luli would set off with Derain, she would go down to the holding cage to watch their unwanted guest, Galena Chadov. Sometimes she would sit and watch her from a distance. Sometimes she would come across Anton doing the same. As the time for the drop off grew closer, Luli decided it was time to have a talk with the woman.

She found a small crate that she could use as a seat. Galena watched without much interest as she pulled the crate over and sat on it. The prisoner sat with her back against one of the cage walls with her knees drawn into her chest. She sat in the small cell as if waiting for her execution.

'*I guess, in a way, she has been,*' Luli thought as she clasped her hands in front of her and looked directly at the prisoner. The hair that had started to grow back along the scar tissue on her head was definitely coming in white. She waited until Galena looked her in the eyes before she dropped them again.

"We aren't going to kill you, you know," said Luli.

Galena's hands crawled up to hold onto her dog tags. She muttered, "You might as well. My 'life' is to be extinguished per court order." Her hands dropped to her lap, "At least if you did it, it would be over and done. Not another side show for the civvies."

Luli watched as Galena's hands crept up to the tags almost as if to make sure they were still there. Luli thought back to how they found her when the Captain knocked her out. She had had the dog tags around her neck even though Derain had taken them from her. She watched her reach up to touch them for a moment before settling her hands back into her lap.

Luli asked, "Why are those tags so important to you? I would think they would be an unpleasant reminder of what you've done."

"You wouldn't understand," she said bitterly in response.

Luli cocked her head and stared at the

woman in the cell, "Try me."

Galena looked away and reached up to touch the tags. "You think of yourself as a person right? Someone who can think and make decisions?" She looked up at Luli, "And you expect to be treated as more than that crate you're sitting on, correct?"

Luli, confused by where the conversation was going, took a moment before she answered, "I do, yes. Why?"

"I was not considered a person. No matter how much I might think that I was or how many times I would try to make decisions for myself. I. Was. Not. A. Person." She looked Luli in the eye and raised the tags up, "Until I was issued these. Until I was given a name." She dropped her hand from the tags as they jingled to her chest. "Because they needed to make up a name to even issue these to a drone... a nonentity." She looked away before she continued, "What you take for granted as a living being in this shit hole of a galaxy, I had to earn. Fight, scratch, claw and bleed for... take lives for. These stupid sheaths of plastic and circuitry are what validate my existence as a person." She wrapped her arms around her knees, "Of course, they remind me of bad times too, but they primarily remind me that I am an entity; not born, but still recognized legally as a being. A being that can make its own decisions." She looked up at Luli, "These are the most valuable things I can own. They are the very first things I actually could own. Hell, these are the only things I still own."

Luli was quiet as she digested everything she had just heard. "I can understand why they are so important to you, but you are right. I can never 'know' what they mean to you."

Galena looked on as the slim Asian woman who smelled of metals and plastics stood up and moved the crate back to where it had been. She nodded as the woman thanked her for the explanation and walked past the man she knew as Rabbit.

His high cheek bones and his raven hair nearly hid his blue eyes. Memories flooded up as she saw the captured soldiers on their knees again. She closed her eyes as she felt her past-self pull the trigger again. She shuddered as the body fell and moved on to the next one. Each remembered recoil, another death on her hands, but another life for the men under her command.

Anton turned as she spoke out loud, "A person who can make decisions, good or bad."

He left the machine room shortly after. He wandered slowly through the gym, out through the hatch to the walkway in the cargo bay. He headed to the lift, but it was on the top deck. He manually opened the doors to the lift. Using the maintenance ladder as an anchor, he floated down to the first deck and forced the doors open. He stepped into the cargo bay proper.

The sickbay hatch was still open and he could hear Barney cursing Doc and Doc's bleating retorts. With a wry smile, he stepped into the sickbay and uttered, "Hate to interrupt your loving epithets, but do you need any help? It's been so long since I've been back on board Matilda here that I'm feeling like a third wheel."

Doc let off a string of mechanical gutturals, snarls and whistles.

Anton laughed, "I'm pretty sure I don't want to know what he said."

"I don't need you just yet, but I will soon." Barney indicated one of the counters in the room, "Why don't you pull up a pew and sit with me until I do."

"I would love to watch you work, Mr. de Lagnel. It is always a pleasure to be in the presence of a master," Anton replied as he sat on the counter. "How far along are you, anyway?"

"I still have to replace the hydraulic line. The tear is just too ragged. There's not enough give for Doc to roam. This is the last cable though," Barney declared, as he continued working.

The three of them sat in relative silence while Barney spliced the damaged cable. Anton finally broke the quiet with, "How bad was it when I left, Barney? Everyone seems to be doing fine, but there is an edginess I feel whenever I'm near anyone that I don't remember being there."

Barney let his hands fall as he looked up at Anton, "It was bad, but you knew that." He turned back to the cable, "You had to go and do what you felt was the right thing and she had to stay and keep Matilda flying; keep the rest of us alive. It was a pretty dry period before we took on the bounty hunter. It opened up more work for us and we changed to meet it." He screwed the connector back onto the end of the cable and tugged on it to make sure it was solidly seated. "You should be asking her, though, not me. Here; give me a hand and reattach this one, would you?"

Anton slipped off the counter, helped Barney up and took the repaired cable. He placed it in his mouth and started scaling Doc. Doc made some complaining beeps, but stopped once he plugged the cable back in. Anton let go and fell back to the deck.

Barney grumbled, "How's that, you old auton. Better?" The robot chirruped in a pleased tone as it ran its arms through a test. "Just have to replace the hydraulic line and then you'll have full mobility in sickbay again."

Barney looked at Anton, "Luli and Derain will be leaving soon to drop off the dead skip. We'll meet back up with them at Chalman's. You have any parting words for Luli? It'll be a couple weeks before we see her again."

"Only that I don't trust that bounty hunter. He's up to something."

"Of course he's up to something, we all are. Each for our own reasons, too. Of course, he doesn't trust you either." Barney paused, "He won't cross us if that's what concerns you. I'm going to get started on this line and get this out of the way as soon as I can. Why don't you go up and see what we're having for dinner."

"I'll do that. I need some time to think anyway," Anton said as he walked through the hatch into the cargo bay.

nine

Ghost Riders in the Sky

Derain and Luli boarded his ship, the Waratah, in the weightless hangar. He had already strapped the body to the deck of the Waratah as Luli ran the pre-flight checks. He took the co-pilot seat and strapped in. They were as prepared for the bounty drop on Caleb's moon as they could be.

Luli nodded at him and said, "Ready for departure, Matilda. Are we clear for takeoff?"

The hangar door rumbled open as the small ship unhooked from the deck to float lazily in the bay. As the door ground to a halt, Jacquie's voice rang over the speaker, "Matilda to Waratah, clear for takeoff. Safe voyage."

Luli replied, "See you in a couple weeks, Matilda. Waratah Out."

She slowly maneuvered the small ship

out of the hangar bay. Once clear of the door, she rode the attitudinal jets to bring her in line with where Caleb's moon would be in less than a solar day. Once the trajectory was locked in, she pushed the burners hot for a brief moment and killed them just as quickly, letting inertia carry them to their destination.

**

Anton monitored their departure through Matilda's tracking system. He glanced at the Captain, "They're away."

She gazed back at him from the communication station, "Do you think you can keep an eye out up here for me? I have to schedule our cargo drop on Chalman's."

After he nodded, she turned back to the station and continued to poll for open slots at the docking port. The ship needed a couple of weeks on planet side for refueling and water alone. The docking charge was going to be huge.

"Even in this backwater system, prices are going up." Disheartened, she sent a message to the Loaders Union on the planet for the pickup on the cargo. She also checked the existing list of merchants still looking for space to ship out on. "Just passenger manifests and some low grade ore shipments. Hopefully we'll have a better selection once we get planet bound."

"I'm sure something will come up,"

responded Anton.

"I really hope so. We've had to settle for some long boring hauls and less than legal deliveries just to make enough mazuma lately. We're keeping our heads above water, but it's been getting tighter and tighter," her hands went up to cradle her chin.

Anton looked at her and saw the worry etched into her face. He turned back to look out the bow port as he whispered, "I'm sorry I haven't been there for you these last few years. Instead of making a difference, looks like I made it harder for everyone." He glanced toward her, "I hope you know that's not what I was trying to do. I just wanted to change things, to make it easier for everyone. Point out a problem that the powers-that-be would notice and fix. Instead I just made it tougher on everyone, including myself." He lamented, "Hurting those I care about in ways I hadn't even thought of."

Jacquie got up and gave Anton a long hug. "We've been doing alright. I'm just glad to have you back with us. Though I am hoping to see that smile of yours before you feel the need to leave us again."

At this moment, Barney's voice crackled over the comm system, "I'm going to need one of you pretty soon. Don't get too involved in anything."

Jacquie broke the hug and clicked the comm, "I'll come down Barney. Just let me know when." She tripped it back off, "You've got her under control, Rabbit? I really need to move around." She stretched and rested her hand on the back of Anton's chair.

"I may be rusty, but I didn't forget everything. If I get stuck, I'll call for you," he told her as she left the bridge.

***

Luli released the stick and let the Waratah go its merry way. It was an older model shock team transport that was designed to seat six, three to a wall with a crew of two. She was fast, heavily armed and armored. The downside was that the cabin didn't have a breathable atmosphere. It always surprised her that Derain owned the ship outright. She had once asked him how he had accomplished that and had gotten some song and dance about a gambling debt and the previous owner being dead. She had learned a long time ago that the best policy was not to pry too hard into his past, especially that story. "We should be at Caleb's in about six hours. Do you know if this is a planet drop or a ship to ship exchange?"

Derain glanced at her as he answered, "They wanted a planet drop. Best to stay fluid, though. Plans in these situations have a tendency to flip flop on a moment's notice." He turned back to the ship's scanners. "Pretty simple plan for now. You'll drop me and the bounty on the moon; then take up a covering position. Should only be one person dirt side with me and only one other ship up. Keep weapons hot, just in case." He looked up at her, "If you think it's going pear shaped, I'll follow your lead on it. I trust your judgment, Lu. Do what you think is best to get both of us out of there with our skin intact. Wouldn't be the first time things went wrong, won't be the last."

***

Barney trundled into the machine room with the roll of damaged tubing over his arm. He set it down and walked over to unspool a new stretch of hydraulic line. He measured the new length out to the centimeter he needed and marked it. Next, he brought it over to the cutter on the bench. As he put it in the clamp, he turned to the woman in the cage, "Of all the cables you ripped out of old Doc, I wish you hadn't torn this one." He closed the cutter and respooled the remnant that wasn't needed. "Messiest job of the week and this tubing isn't getting any easier to find!"

Galena responded, "I'll do better next time."

"There better not be a next time, miss," he retorted. He pulled the connector caps off the old line and secured them to the newly cut one. Once he had finished connecting both caps, he looked directly at her and shook the new line, "If you pull this one out again, I will find you no matter where you are and make you fix it."

Barney turned and spoke into the comm system, "I'll meet one of you two in the med lab. I'm on my way down now."

She watched as the diminutive man rolled the hose up and threw it over his shoulder. His presence had a gravitas that she could feel leave the room as he did. This gave her pause and stopped her from throwing out some passing retort. There was something about him, her brain kept telling her. Given the way he carries himself, he might be from a higher gravity world. Could be very strong, possibly more dangerous than his stature would have you think. Best to keep out of that one's way. She fiddled with the locking mechanism on the cage for the umpteenth time. Feeling beaten, she dropped her hands, "No leaving this box until they open that door."

***

"We're coming up on the moon. Getting a lot of interference on the scanner," Luli said. "Okay. I am getting a ping from a beacon. Heading is locked to it now."

Derain looked out the bow port as the Waratah floated closer to the surface of this little moon. It was a lifeless rock pockmarked with meteor strikes. There would be little to no atmosphere and low gravity. "Head for the beacon, but keep a lookout."

"Coming up on the beacon now. Interference is clearing all of a sudden? Aah, a ship just popped up on the scanner," Luli observed calmly.

"I've made visual with her. Whoa, she's a big one!" Derain exclaimed. "Flash the bow beams three times please." The large ship responded with three flashes back. "Okay Luli, set her down. Pull back up and expect trouble."

Luli slowly brought the Waratah down while she kept a visual on the other vessel as it descended. She brought her ship to within a few meters of the spike beacon, but nothing registered amiss on the ground. Derain stood up, walked over to the closest supply cabinet and pulled out two pistols and an extra belt. He strapped the belt on, strode to the furthest cabinet, and pulled out the body. The body was very light in the low gravity and it hovered briefly before falling slowly as Derain checked his pistols. Satisfied with them, he holstered one, hoisted the body to his shoulder and knocked on the hull.

Luli triggered the rear boarding hatch and Derain hopped out. His landing was punctuated by puffs of dust from his boots as they hit the surface. He watched as the Waratah's hatch closed and lifted straight off on its attitudinal jets. He turned around and watched three figures step off the other ship. That ship pulled up and floated serenely behind the figures. Of the three, one carried a bag and waved three fingers above his head.

"Monitor channel three, Luli," Derain stated as he headed for the beacon. As he moved, the three figures also moved toward it. Two of the figures stopped and took up crossfire positions. Each of them brought up a rifle pointed in Derain's general direction. The man with the bag reached the beacon first and Derain just moments later.

"Hello, Mr. Tiwi. I have heard of you. You may call me Mr. Leon," said the man as he placed the strap to the bag around the upright beacon. "Is that the Doctor you have there?"

Derain released the body, bringing the face into the view of Mr. Leon. "It is. Is that our agreed upon price?"

"It is. It is," replied the man as he stared intently at the face of the corpse that Derain held up by the hair. With a brief flash, a sword flew up into Mr. Leon's hands and decapitated the body, leaving Derain holding just the head. No one moved as the body slowly crumpled to the moon's surface. Mr. Leon sheathed the sword and then indicated the head, "I'll take that, if you please."

He caught the head Derain had released in shock and placed it in a pouch. "I may call upon you again Mr. Tiwi. I bid you good day." Mr. Leon bowed and turned to walk back to his people.

Derain watched as the two others joined Mr. Leon and waited for their ship to descend. He grabbed the bag and backpedaled to his rendezvous point. "Come and get me as fast as you can, Luli." He waited nervously as the Waratah touched down and ran up the ramp. He slapped the door controls as he yelled, "Get us out of here now! As far away as possible." He strode up to the copilot's seat and strapped in.

Luli ran nav coordinates to Chalman's and brought the ship into its path. She gunned it as Derain stared out the bow port. She watched as the tension knotting his frame left him the further they got from the other ship, "Who was that? Derain? Who is Mr. Leon?"

Derain opened the bag and rifled through the various pockets on the inside and outside. It seemed as if he was searching frantically for something and became more concerned when it didn't appear. He grew more agitated as he took the bundles of mazuma apart, "I can't find it. I can't find it." His hands dropped to his lap and the bag fell from his grip. "I really hope that means he was sincere."

"Derain, who is Mr. Leon and what are you looking for?" asked Luli.

He stopped and stared at her a moment before he responded, "Mr. Leon? Mr. Leon is a very dangerous man. A very powerful, dangerous man. People don't just meet him. The people who do, have a tendency to not be heard from again." He put the bundles back together. "I was looking for a bomb or tracking device, but it looks like the bag is clean. I am going to try to relax now," he expressed as he released a pent up breath. "Let's get to Chalman's world and get out of this accursed system."

ten

Straighten Up and Fly Right

"Matilda, you are clear to land. Dock at Port 327-B for your two week layover," came over the comm system.

"Roger tower, cleared for landing. Docking at Port 327-B," replied Jacquie. She brought the Matilda down into a controlled glide until she sighted the port. "See if you can get our haulers on the line as soon as we're down, Anton." She angled the ship over their docking port and brought it in smoothly. She killed the engines and started the shutdown procedure. "Barney, bring the engines down for long storage. We'll be here a while."

"Roger, Captain," Barney responded over the comm system.

Anton started to speak with the

Loaders Union requesting cargo pickup. He turned to the Captain, "It's a no go, Jacq. We'll have to take it to them."

"Bloody unions. The same on every planet," She keyed the comm, "Barney, prep for a dust and rush." She turned to Anton, "Rabbit, you remember how to drive the runner?" At his nod, "Get her prepped then." She stood up and walked to the hatch, "I have to make some special arrangements. Meet you in the bay."

"Understood, Captain," Anton said as he cleared the nav station and headed out right behind her. It had been a long time since he'd driven the spider runner.

The spider runner was a twelve meter long, four legged crawler built with an encased cabin for worlds with caustic atmospheres or no atmosphere at all. It had three wheels on a spindle on each leg; each one was for different terrain. Even the cabin could withstand being submerged in a liquid environment. Its towing capacity was set for two forty meter shipping containers loaded to bear, which was what the Matilda carried attached to the aft section. It was a strange looking vehicle that was best suited for variable terrain. Most ports had paved runs, but some of the backwaters still had dirt, rock or worse for cargo drops. Chalman's had a little of both. He ran the diagnostics on the crawler and everything came on green. The engine kicked on as he tripped the runner to ship comm, "Barney, are we at de-latch?"

Barney's voice came through, "Aye. You ready for the hitch up?"

"On my way now," replied Anton.

Jacquie stood at the cargo bay door controls with a data pad in her hand. She keyed the bay doors open and walked over to the runner. Anton felt the runner shift as she stepped on the side rail, rapped on the window and gave him the thumbs up. The crawler started forward as the front two legs swung outward and the rear legs shifted forward. He drove the runner through the bay doors and angled it to the right to go around the side of the ship. The Matilda's two landing legs were out and her chin rested in the dirt of this planet. Anton kept the runner walking past the Matilda until he could see the two shipping containers hanging from underneath the flight deck. He brought the runner around so that it was facing forward and away from the containers.

"We need to give this thing a name," Anton stated.

Barney chimed in, "Oh, we did while you were gone. It's called Rabbit's Folly. Didn't anyone tell you?"

"Hardy har," muttered Anton as Jacquie's laughter rang out over the comm channel. He felt the Rabbit's Folly shift as she dropped off the rail to the ground.

Jacquie asked, "Repulsors active on both, Barney?" She waited for the affirmative before she gave the order, "Drop right."

The forty meter long shipping container on the starboard side of the tail rack of the ship detached. The repulsor field on the bottom of the container cushioned the fall and it hovered a few feet off the ground. Jacquie walked over to it and waved to Anton to back up the Folly. Once it was close, she latched it to the rear of the runner and waved it forward. Anton pulled the runner up until the back end of the container was just past the lower back end of the Matilda.

"Barney, drop the left," came over the comm.

Barney had waited patiently at the manual latch control for the other container in the main shaft of the ship. He pulled the latch and felt the release of the container as a deep thump. He reset the latch mechanisms for both sides and then headed up to the top deck. Just as he entered the hatch to the bridge, he heard, "The ship is all yours. Lock her down for now."

Barney flipped the comm, "Order received, Matilda out." He triggered the cargo bay doors shut. "Now, what to do with myself for a couple weeks?"

Jacquie triggered the comm off as she sat in the passenger seat of the crawler. She looked down at the data pad and ordered, "Head to Warehouse A-15 for the rear container. Then we'll move onto Warehouse D-6 for the first one."

Anton started the runner forward and they rode on quietly as Jacquie scrolled through the available outbound cargo lists. He heard her grumble in frustration as she closed the list down.

"Slim pickings still. Keep your fingers crossed for a big job coming in within the next couple of weeks." She peered out the bow port, "That's the one we're looking for. Don't see the dock manager anywhere. Looks like they've left us waiting."

Jacquie stepped out and signaled to Anton where to leave the container until the manager showed up. As the Folly came to a stop, Anton stepped out to join Jacquie on the rail of the runner. They shared one of the drink rations stowed on the crawler.

They didn't have to wait long before a woman sporting coveralls with the docking company's logo on it came around the bend. Jacquie slid off the rail and walked over to the lady with her data pad in hand.

"Hello. I am Representative Aviles of the docking office. Your name and delivery order ID?" asked the woman.

"Captain Jacquotte Delahaye of the Matilda and delivery order 7515-300," she replied.

"Sign here and here," Ms. Aviles directed. After both boxes were signed, the manifest on Jacquie's data pad lit up as 'Arrived'.

"We're off to D-6, Ms. Aviles. Did you need a lift?" asked Jacquie.

She poured over her manifests before she looked up at the Captain. She thought a moment before she responded "I'll take you up on that ride. Sure beats walking. I have a few other stops, but they can wait."

"Hop on. We'll try to get out of your hair as soon as we can," replied Jacquie. All three of them piled into the crawler and headed toward Warehouse D-6.

As they rode along, the dock representative said, "Thanks for the lift. Sometimes all the walking can get pretty punishing."

"We were headed over there anyway. You guys seem to be pretty busy today," Anton piped up.

"Today. This week. We're expecting a lot more deliveries in for the next couple of weeks." Ms. Aviles looked questioningly at the Captain, "Are you flying out soon?"

"We haven't found anything worth shipping yet so we're stuck here for a bit," fretted Jacquie.

"Yeah, outgoing is pretty light right now." She glanced out the bow port, "Looks like we're here."

The Captain and the dock representative kept talking as they exited the crawler in front of Warehouse D-6. Anton backed the other container into the warehouse as Jacquie signed off on the delivery.

Before they made ready to leave, Jacquie asked Ms. Aviles, "Do you need a lift to your next stop?"

"My next stop is actually just a couple slots down." She paused a moment, "You know what? You can call me Marta. You'll be here at port for a while?" After the Captain nodded, she continued, "I'll keep an eye out for any big deliveries. The Matilda, right?"

"Thanks, Marta. The Matilda, yes."

Anton watched as Jacquie shook hands with Marta and waited for her to board as Marta moved on to her next delivery point. After Jacquie was comfortably seated, Anton quipped, "And that's how you grease a squeaky wheel, eh?"

"Shush, you. Giving someone a lift is not taking advantage of them. Besides, it didn't cost us anything, but kindness." Jacquie pulled a map up on her data pad, "Okay, last drop off. We're going to wait until Luli and Derain are back for it." She looked hard at Anton, "We might need backup."

eleven

Beauty and Stupid

The Waratah lighted on the flight deck before maneuvering into the hangar. Luli and Derain had made better time than expected and had returned within the week.

Marta had given the Captain the hookup on one delivery already. It was a high value drop to the Spur system; Zangspur to be exact. It was a short trip as well; only one jump gate. The Captain still needed to find a second haul to the same system, but nothing had pulled up except a passenger manifest. Jacquie was accepting the consignment as Luli and Derain walked onto the bridge.

"Easy delivery?" asked Derain.

Jacquie looked up, "Yes. And you?"

"Nothing went awry, if that's what

you mean." He dropped the bag onto the station top.

"I'm going to get cleaned up," Luli said, giving Jacquie a hug before she left the bridge.

"Nothing went awry, huh?" the Captain said dryly.

"The buyer was someone I've only heard of by reputation." He paused a moment, "It went smoothly." It felt good to be back on board. "Any problems with our guest?"

"She's been quiet. I still have one other drop off to make, but I think that having back up on hand would be the smart decision. Think you can be ready soon?"

"You know me, Captain. Give me the when and where and I'll be there," rattled Derain.

She rolled her eyes at him, "I will when I know it. To keep you in the loop, we're heading to the Spur system next."

"Thanks. I'll keep an eye out." He pulled out a few stacks of the mazuma in the bag and handed it to the Captain, "Your cut. I already gave Luli hers and I'm off to see Barney next. Then I'm going to get myself cleaned up."

"Thanks for this. This'll help cover the replacement of essentials. Can you believe I'm still waiting for payment from one of the cargo drops?" She sat back in the chair, "We'll be leaving in five planetary days, which works out to just shy of 150 hours. Can you get your other bounty drop-off for our guest set up in that time?"

"I'll work on it as soon as I'm cleaned up." He headed for the hatch, "Anything else, Captain?" After she shook her head in the negative, he bowed gracefully and left the bridge.

The Captain rang down to Luli's cabin. "Luli, do you think you can get a gig at one of the local dives?"

Luli stepped out of the fresher and keyed the comm, "What was that, Captain?"

"We need a cover for one of our trades. Do you think you can get a gig at one of the local dives?"

"I think Harry still runs the Jump Jacks out here. I'll find out." Luli fell back onto her bed, "Let me catch some shut eye, Jacq. Out."

***

Everyone met up later that night in the lounge. The Captain had given Anton some currency to buy some clothes as it hadn't taken long before he had burned his prison uniform. Derain had been forced to lend him some clothes in the meantime and he was still not happy about that. Anton felt that he 'owed' the crew, so he had purchased some local produce and made dinner for everyone. He said it was thanks for getting him off the Vogelgesang.

"Once I start pulling my own mazuma, I'll repay you, Jacq," he announced over everyone's eating.

Jon Gray Lang

"You keep cooking like this, and I'll pay to keep you onboard," Luli said around a mouthful.

Barney sat back and rubbed his belly, "Aah, it's good to have you back. I'd forgotten food could taste delicious."

"This must be the reason the Captain wanted to rescue you," Derain laughed.

"It's all in the ingredients. You can only do so much with food cubes," Anton explained. "I'm sure you'll all think less of me once the good protein runs out."

As the meal drew to a close, Jacquie stated, "Everyone, listen up. We already have one shipping container reattached to the hull. We'll be getting a passenger container in the next couple of days." She waved down the disagreements and continued, "I know, I know. I'm not happy about it either, but it's what we've got. The passengers know they won't have access to the ship, so it should be an uneventful trip. We still have two other deliveries left to take care of while we're here, though. Luli, did you get a show at the Jump Jack?"

"Harry passed away, but his son recognized me. He renamed the club the Blink Tank. I'll be playing tomorrow night. How big is the shipment?" Luli asked.

"Just a crate. It's already on board the Folly. I'll call our buyer and set up the meet for tomorrow night. That leaves the bounty for our guest. Derain?" asked the Captain.

"They've given me a time, but I am still waiting for a location." He picked up his glass, "Let's shoot for an uneventful delivery... on both."

***

With the dawn of the next day, Derain had received a location for the exchange on the genorg. The destination had been given as a latitude, longitude point.

"The drop off is in the middle of nowhere. It's pretty far out from port," asserted Derain. "Smells like trouble."

"Have to agree. We're going to need everyone on this. You willing to step up, Rabbit?" asked the Captain. "Any help would be appreciated."

Anton looked up slowly from his fiddling hands, "I'll help. What to do you need me to do?"

Jacquie replied, "We'll figure something out. In the meantime, let's see what we can do to get the water and fuel tanks topped off today and help Luli get prepped for tonight."

Anton got up from the table in the ship's lounge as the chorus of 'aye' died down. He stepped onto the lift and got off at the second deck. Galena watched him walk in to the machine room with a preoccupied look on his face. He was still young looking, possibly twenties to early thirties, though age was hard to measure nowadays. Time dilation made the judging of age difficult, especially for travelers. He still had that rakish half smile, but he looked more worn than she remembered. Jail time had not treated him well. He was leaner, his movements almost feline. She couldn't look away as he paced back and forth in front of her.

It was strange. Of all the prisoners Galena had captured on Tigron, his face stayed clear in her mind. The dead and the living from that day had mostly become a blur in her memories, but he always remained in focus. She had no idea what had happened to him after she transferred those enemy combatants to someone else's care, not even when she herself had been relieved of command. He kept appearing in her dreams, even as he had slipped from her conscious thought. But when she saw him on the loading dock for the prison ship, it had felt like the next day. So strange. She looked up and jerked back in surprise as he stood against the bars of her cage staring at her in return.

"Why are you here?" he glared at her. "How did you, in all of blasted space, end up on the same prison ship as me? As all of the ones that you let live? Some kind of cosmic joke?" He looked away for a moment then turned to face her with a very serious expression, "We're going to turn you over tomorrow. As of right now it sounds like it's going to be a bad deal for you; maybe for us. I still don't know how I feel about that; about you." He wandered over to a worktable and gripped it hard. "I see your face... those eyes in my dreams... in my

Jon Gray Lang

nightmares." He turned quickly and ran to her cage and shook the bars violently, "Why did you choose to keep me alive? Why me?" His hands dropped to his sides, "I can't figure it out. What made me more important than Johnson, Henry or any of the rest?"

Galena quieted for a moment before she responded, "I, I don't have a good answer for you. Nothing with any meaning. You were just far enough down the line. Simple as that."

Anton had a defeated look on his face as if he already knew that was the answer. "Then why did you keep me alive back on Tigron? Why did you keep me from getting murdered for my food ration? Why then?"

She looked thoughtful before she answered, "I don't know. I recognized you. I didn't recognize them. Seeing a familiar face in trouble? Someone I could help? I don't know."

They both stood there in silence, each with their own thoughts, their own memories. Finally, Anton turned toward the door to leave.

Galena said to his back, "Thanks for freeing me from the prison ship. Thanks for letting me live a little longer."

"One debt, repaid." He walked through the hatch and out of her view.

***

Hours later, Galena watched as the stern looking, tall black man with his hair tied back,

Jon Gray Lang

walked over and locked the hatch to the machine room. She heard him say 'clear' through the intercom and then lock the hatch to the gym. All of the lights around her shut off except for a small one on the workbench. She felt a rumble through the floor and then another rumble.

"Great," she muttered. "Just me and my thoughts for another night."

***

The crew of the Matilda boarded the crawler, recently christened Rabbit's Folly, bound for the Blink Tank. They would finish up a bit of smuggling and then would sit back to enjoy a show played by their pilot, Luli Qing. The talk on board the crawler was jovial. Everyone was lighthearted, even Anton, who had seemed morose earlier in the day. Luli stepped into the club in this backwater port and the rest of them spread out as she negotiated with the new owner for her cut of the evening.

Strange as it may sound, Luli was pretty well known as a musician throughout most of the systems that made up the Consortium. Other systems outside of that, too, if you believed her. Deep spacers had a strange, almost legendary status amongst the populations of the colonies. Technically, everyone out here owed one deep spacer or another, their very existence.

Since the end of the twenty first

century, humanity had begun its major push into outer space. Faster-Than-Light travel had not been invented yet, so sleeper ships were sent out into the cosmos.

Planets that were able to sustain life had been found such as Malina, Sihnon, and Carpathia. There were problems during this early colonization period, though. The Tellus colony led to war which had devastated the Sol system. Other planets, such as LV-426 and G889 were found to be important scientific discoveries or horrific mistakes.

By the twenty third century, the Sol system was as fully occupied as it would ever become. The earth had been left a ruin and the mass exodus of humanity hit its stride. New systems were discovered and new technologies increased the exodus. Communications between these new and old populated systems broke down. Eventually all touch was lost with the home system. Few remember the Sol system now and even fewer know where it was. Those few are the living deep spacers.

By the time of the discovery of various forms of FTL travel, humanity had spread to the stars and lost itself. FTL travel had allowed the humans in the Malina system to expand and take over other settled systems. Eventually this led to the Consortium controlled systems. Over a century ago, deep spacers were sought after for their knowledge of other settled systems. Once that knowledge had been passed on many of those old spacers were never heard from again... and Consortium controlled space grew. That's no longer the case, in the twenty-ninth century. There are so few deep space pilots left that they are well known and well loved by the populace. Sometimes it made life difficult, sometimes it was too easy. At last count, only about eight pilots were left and all of them were considered to be ancient.

Luli had little trouble negotiating her time with the club once word spread she would be there. It was a packed house she played to later that night.

Barney took up a position in the far corner as Anton set up at the bar. Jacquie and Derain pulled up to a table with a couple of empty chairs at it. The lights were turned down low as Luli stepped onto the stage. There was some clapping as she thanked the audience for coming. Then she pulled out her made-from-actual-Earth-wood ukulele and she glowed within the stage lights.

Luli addressed the audience, "This instrument was given to me by my father as a gift for my first deep space piloting job. It had been in my family for generations, ever since the first Qings left old Earth and settled in the Asteroid Belt. He knew he would be long dead by the time I returned. I remember it well. I cried when he handed it to me. The last thing he ever said to me was, play it with all your heart and I'll hear it no matter where I am." She paused for a moment, "Please join me as I play for my family on the other side of life's journey."

Jon Gray Lang

Anton sat and listened to her sing. It's funny the things that you miss until they are gone. He relaxed as he finally felt at home for the first time in many years. He continued to watch her when he spied two gentlemen who made a beeline to Jacquie and the bounty hunter.

Barney gave the two men a cursory glance and noted they were both armed. He recognized them as long term middle men that the Captain had done business with many times before. It never hurt to expect trouble, though. He didn't get a sense of any tenseness so he went back and listened to Luli play. But he kept the men in his peripheral.

Luli, like many deep spacers had taken to music on her long journeys. For months, the pilot would be the only person on board a sleeper ship who was awake. To hear any voice, including your own could help stave off the eventual loneliness. It would almost seem strange that hobbies from the old sailing ship days would become prevalent in the early days of space travel. However, there was very little to do once the course was plotted out and that meant lots of downtime. On very rare occasions, some of the deep space pilots would end up in the same port. When this happened, they would play together until their individual ships left.

The crowd sat enraptured while Luli was in the moment. These performances made an almost perfect meeting time for the transfer of smuggled goods. Jacquie spoke just loud enough to be heard at the table, "It's good to see you again, Viktor. Did you or Stan order drinks yet?" She raised her hand to grab the attention of the wait staff. Once a waitress came over, she ordered a round of spirits for the table. "Let's celebrate on living another day, eh Vik?"

"Salud!" Viktor Salenov, local contact for the crime syndicate on Chalman's World, raised his drink and nodded. He tipped his glass back and emptied it one swallow. "Still traveling with the bounty hunter, eh? Don't you think he might take you in for a bounty, eventually? You must be wanted somewhere. If not for a crime, then for your beauty, eh? Isn't that right, bounty hunter?"

Stanislav Tenden, Viktor's constant companion didn't touch his drink as Derain lifted his and saluted Viktor and drank half of it. "Nothing on the net right now. But you never know when that cold and rainy day may come."

"I like this one, Jacquie. You should keep him," chuckled Viktor. "But we are here for business. The time for pleasantries is done. You have what I am waiting for?"

"You have what I am waiting for, too?" asked Jacquie. "At the previously agreed upon price?"

"Of course, of course. We have been friends a long time, Captain. A long time." He took Stanislav's drink and downed it in one shot. "It is hard to keep trust for those you work with in this business, yes? When times are easy, people will steal for greed. When times are tough, people will steal for food. The only constant is the stealing." He rubbed his forehead, "But you have not stolen from me nor I from you. This means we have trust, eh?"

"As much as can be had these days," she responded, almost wistfully.

"Trust is a rare commodity, Captain. I hope you cherish it as much as I do." Viktor looked away before he continued, "Stanis, follow the young gentleman out, please. I will stay with the beautiful Captain. Now, where were we? Yes, more drinks!"

Derain left the table and was soon followed by Stanislav out the door of the establishment. They met in the lot outside the club and walked to the crawler. Derain opened the side panel and slid out a rather large, hard case. He cracked the top and stepped back to allow Stanislav access to look inside.

"All in order, Stan?" asked Derain.

Stanislav just looked at him as he keyed his comm device, "Everything is as it should be."

Both men waited a few minutes before Derain received a pulse signal that he knew was the all clear. He pulled the case out and handed it to Stan. He followed the man to another vehicle, while attempting to make small talk to no avail. As they headed back into the club, one of the local police officers approached, looking as if he might stop them.

"Can't a man meet another man in a parking lot anymore?" shouted Derain. "It's becoming impossible to meet folks anywhere these days!"

The police officer stopped, looked a bit confused then backed up and walked the other way.

Stanislav held the door open, but blocked Derain from entering. He uttered in a flat voice, "Mr. Leon sends his regards." He then stepped in while a flustered Derain stood outside as the door shut in his face. The bounty hunter composed himself, opened the door and stepped back into the club. He made a beeline to sit with Barney.

Luli finished out her first set, thanked the crowd and went to the bar to sit with Anton. "As good as you remember it?"

"Better actually." He flagged the bartender down, "A drink for the lovely lady." He waited while the drink was placed in front of her. "Still feel good to play in front of all these people?"

"Always," she said with a twinkle in her eye. "I love these moments of being surrounded by people after a long trip. Makes me feel human. Hey! Don`t forget to take it easy tonight. We have a busy morning."

"Oh, I remember. Are you doing another set?"

"That`s the plan anyway." She took a

long pull on her drink, "You staying for it?"

"Most like."

She gave him a brief hug, "Thanks for the drink!" she chirped and headed back toward the stage.

Anton spied Barney and the bounty hunter in deep conversation while Jacquie laughed at something Viktor had said. "No matter how much things change, they always stay the same."

The evening progressed without incident and Luli got mobbed at the end of the show. Later, everyone but Jacquie got on board the crawler and headed back to the Matilda. All but Derain got off the runner at the ship. He gave some excuse of checking out the drop site for tomorrow and left.

As the Folly drove away, Anton asked, "Are he and the Captain an item?"

"Maybe once. But not anymore. You jealous?" Barney responded with a leer.

"You know I love her. She's more like a sister to me, though. I'm just concerned is all," Anton bit back.

"She can look after herself, Rabbit. She's been doing it for years," Luli said offhandedly as she walked on board.

"I know. Doesn't mean I can't be worried," Anton groused.

"I worry too, lad. I worry too." Barney patted him on the back, "Good night to the both of you."

"Night Barney, night Anton," Luli gave each of them a peck on the cheek.

"Night guys." Anton dithered for a few moments before he headed up to the machine room.

Galena was asleep when he walked in, but she woke with a start. She watched him as he moved about the machine room. He was sporting a knife now and some new clothes. He finally settled, picked up a small crate and set it down next to her cage, her latest prison. It seemed that she had lived her entire life in a cage and would be trading this one for another tomorrow. What was the old saying? Such is life. Yes, such is life; the life of a drone.

Anton fidgeted with his hands for a while before he said, "I am not fully behind turning you over tomorrow, but I can`t disagree with their decision." He watched her stare mutely back at him before he continued, "I have a very bad feeling, though, that tomorrow is going to go poorly for you." He looked away, "I want to help you for some reason, but I don't want to screw my friends over to do it. I am in a quandary." He sat there and stared at her for a long time before he stood up, put the crate back and left the room.

"What the hell was that about?" she asked the darkness.

twelve

Rebel, Rebel

The next day dawned into a clear morning. The ship was a hive of activity. Derain had come back in the middle of the night and the Captain had shown up in the morning with a bit of a hangover. It didn't slow Jacquie down at all, but she was crabbier than usual.

The air control laws for this rock were pretty stringent, so the Folly would be the vehicle of choice for this job. Derain had checked out the site earlier that night and had stated that there wasn't enough of a clearing out there to land the Waratah anyway. The trade would happen in an overgrown, wooded area. He had called everyone in on this, even Anton. Anton had already let it be known he wouldn't be cut out of this transaction even though he wasn't for it.

Barney and Anton brought Galena down the lift and chained her to a wall in the back of the runner. As Barney stepped away to pick up his 'case of trouble' as he called it, Anton slipped a small knife into Galena's hands.

He whispered, "For you to help yourself."

She nodded in thanks, a little confused by this, but willing to take hope in the gesture. She made space for the oblong box with straps that the small man set on the floor board.

The Captain looked around, "Everyone ready? Let's move." She took her place at the controls and started the engine. The others scrambled on board as the vehicle edged out of the ship and onto the main throughway. The loud thump of the closing cargo doors echoed behind them as they headed out for their last delivery on Chalman's World.

The drive through the port town was short and the wilderness of the planet came on fast and thick. It wasn't a terribly long drive out into the country, but the destination was far enough away that the town wouldn't hear anything if things did indeed go pear shaped. The plan was to get to the meeting site early and prepare for the worst.

The location was a small clearing in the scrub trees. Everyone disembarked the runner, except for Barney and Luli. Luli hopped into the driver's seat and drove the runner around the perimeter. Barney pulled out a series of sensors and placed them at a 100 meter distance around the center of the small clearing. He set them up in such a way that they weren't easily visible. Once he was satisfied with the number of sensors, he linked the sensors up to his wrist pad. He keyed it in and the sensor map came up for the group.

"Sensors up and feed running," stated Barney.

Jacquie checked her wrist pad, "Got it. You two scatter. Anton? Derain? You're with me."

Barney pulled a long barreled rifle out of his 'case of trouble', nodded to Luli and headed for a good vantage point of the area.

Luli took the Folly further back into the scrub trees and activated the turret cannon on the roof of the crawler. She keyed in the sensor feed to the runner's systems. Everyone felt that this was going to go south so all the stops had been pulled. As Barney had said, "Three clean jobs in a row? There's gonna be one hell of a pay-back and soon."

Galena fingered the knife that Anton had given her and watched the ship's crew set up. The bronze skinned woman with the golden eyes who she had taken her tags from acted as the leader of the team. She definitely wore the leadership role as one accustomed to it.

Galena watched Anton fiddle with his borrowed pistol as the Captain spoke with the tall black man. "That must be the bounty hunter," she considered quietly. She heard the runner come to a stop and heard the diminutive man's voice concerning a sensor net. For a simple bounty drop, they did seem to be expecting trouble. Unless they were this prepared all the time. They had responded pretty quickly when she had gotten loose from their sickbay now that she thought back on it. She continued to watch them from her crouched position. The Captain and the bounty hunter conversed while Rabbit kept an eye on her. They all settled in for the wait. She fingered the knife again and felt along the bond as it cut into her wrists.

Barney's voice came through on the group channel, "Sensor tripped south, southwest."

Derain stated shortly after, "Incoming message." He keyed to a different channel before he said, "Hello. This is Derain Tiwi. I have your fugitive at the requested coordinates." He nodded briefly, "We will await your arrival." He keyed back to the group channel, "One ship. Incoming."

As the high pitched whine of the ship came over the trees, Barney took a deep breath and let it out slowly. Luli manually directed the turret toward the ship as it hovered over the clearing. Anton holstered his pistol and crossed his arms. Jacquie and Derain spread out in a rather nonchalant manner.

Eight ropes fell through the rapidly opening door from the bottom of the hovering ship. Eight people slid down the ropes and took up positions, leaving two in the center. Anton stared hard and blinked back in recognition, "Sam? Is that you?"

"Hello, Rabbit. Told you we'd see each other again," Sam remarked. "Once my crew picked me up from the Vogelgesang, I put out a bounty on the sweet Lieutenant's head." He made an indication toward Derain, "I can smell a hunter a mile away. Besides having to gut that old prison ship and killing all the prisoners off, the rest, as they say, was cake."

"You spaced everyone on board?" cried Anton.

Sam stated, "Covering an escape is messy business, Roane. Captain, I actually have no interest in your drone there. I want that one, Anton Roane." He paused for effect, "Here's the mazuma as promised. Take it and be on your way. Let's make this easy." The familiar looking woman standing next to him threw a small case toward Jacquie.

Galena sawed at the band that trapped her wrists together and stood up quickly. '*Maybe too fast,*' she thought to herself as she felt the blood rush into her head. "I should've eaten more." She started to move toward the Captain.

Luli spoke into the group channel at this very moment, "Readings coming from the ship! Looks like weapons are powering up!" She kicked on the turret's systems and locked onto the ship.

As Luli's voice faded over the channel, Barney chose one of the eight targets on the ground and pulled the trigger on his rifle. Anton yanked his pistol out and started blasting. Derain backpedaled and unholstered his pistol. The ship's guns melted the ground where the Captain had stood before Galena had rocketed into her. They landed in a heap as a man who had been standing behind Sam crumpled to the ground.

Barney sucked in a deep breath and took aim at the next of the now seven targets and fired. Luli released a shot toward the hovering ship from the coil gun turret. Derain brought his pistol to bear and shot into the quickly spreading group of adversaries. One fell to the ground. Anton cracked another shot that hit Sam in the gut. As Sam stumbled backward, Rosa, the woman standing next to him, fired from the hip. Derain cried out and fell to his knees. A heavy shot rang out from the trees and smashed into the ship. Anton turned his head to track the origin of the shot and felt an impact in his right arm. As he spun around, he saw another man fall to the ground.

The ship started to list as another accelerated round impacted the ship's frame. Galena rolled off the Captain with her wrists free and the knife in her hand. She spun and ran toward the closest enemy to her. The Captain rolled over, brought her pistol out and blew the kneecap off of one of the running assailants. He screamed as he crumpled. While she tracked him, she noticed the case lying on the ground close to her. She reached out a hand to grab it and jerked back from a round blasting the case. She looked over in time to see the head of the man who had shot at her explode.

She grabbed the case and keyed the group channel, "Pull back! Pull back!" She stood up just as the genorg leapt out and cut the neck of a man who had been shooting at her crew. Blood sluiced through the air and the genorg grabbed the rifle from the falling body. She brought it to bear on a woman who fired at Anton. "Lieutenant, pull back!" she cried out.

Barney took another shot before he packed up the rifle and dropped from his vantage point. The familiar woman from the prison ship had moved quickly, so he had only nicked her in the leg. He two-timed it back to the Folly. "I'm gonna miss those sensors."

Luli fired another round toward the ship through the coil gun, but the pilot had finally taken the hint. It had tracked her shots to zero in on her trajectory. She heard the door swing open and watched Barney's box fly unceremoniously to the floor boards.

"I'm going to have to adjust the damn seat, you giant bastards!" cried Barney as Luli's laughter rolled in the background. He started the runner up and drove back to the clearing. "Not sure, but I think a couple of ours got hit. Be ready!"

Galena heard the Captain's call as the attacking ship's cannon started blowing the clearing to pieces. She turned to watch Anton and the Captain grab the downed bounty hunter and shuffle off into the woods. She turned tail and ran after them.

The ship gave chase as Rosa checked on the man Rabbit called Sam. Jacquie and the rest piled into the runner as Galena ran up behind them. She heard the turret go off and a moment later the sound of tearing metal reached her ears. The ship was right on top of them! She dove into the crawler and felt arms grab her and pull her in. The door slammed shut and the Folly lurched crazily away from the clearing. She heard the small man's voice ring out, "I can barely see over the bloody dashboard! I'm doing the best I can!"

"Anton! Med kit!" screamed Jacquie as she tabbed the seat adjuster for Barney.

"Thanks love!" he cried as the seat configured to his body.

Anton scrabbled for the med kit until he found it and pulled it free. Galena ripped it out of his hands as the runner tipped to the right.

"Luli! How we doing?" yelled Jacquie.

The whine of the coil gun in the turret rang in the cabin before Luli responded, "That ship is gaining, but listing pretty badly!"

Galena tore open the med kit and helped prep the bounty hunter with Anton's help. She wrapped a quick tourniquet around his leg above the hole and tore the pant leg open. Jacquie leaned over and started cleaning the wound. Derain, at this point had passed out and Anton was leaning heavily against the side panel of the Folly, looking pale himself.

The coil gun whine rang out in the cabin again and then Luli cheered, "She's losing altitude! She's hitting the trees! Oh my!"

They all felt the crawler rock to the explosion just behind them. The ship careened off course and slammed into the ground in a fiery blast. Luli dropped to the deck and pulled Anton's sleeve away from his wound. As Galena and the Captain finished with Derain, they both went to work on Anton.

"Barney, slow it down once we get near town. No need to gather attention to ourselves," said Jacquie. She looked hard at Galena as she finished binding Anton's wounds. "You're pretty good in a fight, for a drone. Even better as a field medic."

Galena glared at the Captain as she cleaned her hands. She passed the cleaning supplies over to Luli. "You can call me by my name or as Lieutenant... not drone, not genorg. Got it?"

Jacquie raised her hands in mock surrender, "Understood."

Barney brought the crawler into the cargo bay of the Matilda and closed the doors. The three ladies carried Derain and Anton into the sickbay. After they were secured, Luli headed up top deck.

Jacquie and Barney brought out solvents and began to clean the inside of the Folly. Eventually, Galena joined them. Once that was done, the crawler was secured to the deck.

Luli's voice rang out over the ships comm, "Captain? The Loaders Union is waiting on us for our final pickup. Umm, a passenger manifest?"

Jacquie grunted, "Tell them we can link it up now. We need to get out of here before someone finds that crashed ship in the forest."

"Aye, aye Captain. Message relayed," Luli laughed.

"Passengers, huh? Fun," said Barney. "I'll be up at the clips for the container." He headed toward the lift after the short nod from Jacquie. He wondered what the Captain was going to do with the Lieutenant. But that was up to her. Good thing, too. That girl knew how to handle herself. If the decision was his, she would get to stay on board.

As Barney wandered off, Jacquie picked up the case that she had grabbed from the clearing. She walked it over to one of the crates of foodstuffs secured to the floor and finagled the lock. She popped it open and an 'Oh' escaped her lips.

Galena walked over to see what was inside and watched as the Captain counted out 6 huge stacks of mazuma. The Captain clipped each stack and placed all but one back in the case. She turned around and offered her the clip she had left out.

"I'll say this for Anton's friend. He was willing to pay," said the Captain. "Your cut."

Galena stared dumbly at it in

confusion.

Jacquie waved the mazuma in front of her, "Your cut. You earned it." She finally gave up and just stuffed it into the genorg's hands... the Lieutenant's hands she corrected herself. "By the way, I am Jacquotte Delahaye and this is my ship, the Matilda. And what is your name, Lieutenant?"

Galena was quiet a moment. She didn't understand what was going on. Her face hardened and she snapped out a salute, "I am Lieutenant Galena Chadov discharged of the Consortium Military... uh, Captain."

Jacquie waited until the salute died away before she asked, "How would you like a job?"

thirteen

All the Rockets Go Bang

The Matilda left the planet of Chalman's World on schedule with a course set for the local jump gate. The Loaders Union had come through under the clock and had gotten the passenger container on board in record time. Barney had shown Galena how the container latches worked and she had completed her first on board task as the newest member of the crew.

Needless to say, Derain was not happy with her recent inclusion as a crew member, but Barney and Luli both had accepted her with alacrity. Anton had been a touch more ambivalent. The first dinner of the journey to the Spur system was more strained than usual. This was especially odd since they had been paid what they expected; had new cargo and no one had died.

Jon Gray Lang

Anton mended his newly blasted shirt, complained that he had just gotten it and how it was already ruined. Luli and Jacquie had lent Galena some clothes with the promise of a shopping trip on Zangspur.

"Zangspur is a pretty big port planet. Lots of traffic through there as the Spur system is one of the founding systems of the Consortium," Jacquie told Galena. "Finding you some clothes will be easy. We'll make a day of it." She jotted something down on her data pad, "We should get you an atmo suit too. The old ones on board aren't meant for someone of your build. Trust me, I know."

Derain swiveled toward Barney as he wired up some new sensors, and grouched, "I still can't believe I missed most of the fight."

"It was messy, but we got it done." Barney glanced back, "I still can't believe you weren't expecting a double cross. You're paranoid enough for the whole damn boat." He stopped soldering one of the wires, "Did you know that the contact was that Sam fellow?"

"I spoke with the woman, Rosa Keri," assured Derain.

"Did you know she was the same woman who was traveling with that guy?" Barney waited for the small negative, "Shocking. All the pretty ladies look and sound the same, right?"

Derain argued, "Everything sounded on the up and up. Good shooting by the way."

Galena watched as Luli used some form of finger strengthening device. "What is that?" she asked.

"This?" replied Luli. "It's to strengthen my fingers for playing. Do you want to try it?"

"I know if my fingers got any stronger, I'd never leave the ship," quipped Jacquie.

Luli gave her a look over the laughter in the background and turned back to Galena, "Give it a shot."

Galena took the device and stared at it, noticing the four plungers. She placed her hand on it and worked through them individually. "My smallest finger is weak." She handed it back to Luli, "What do you mean by 'playing'? Playing what?"

"Why my music, of course."

Galena sat and thought for a moment before she responded in a flat tone, "The mathematical arrangement of sound and silence. But what is it for? What purpose does it serve?"

"What is music for?" Luli asked, taken aback.

Everyone at the table turned toward Galena and stared at her quizzically. She looked around before dropping her gaze to her lap. *'How like the drone you are to seek to escape standing out,'* she thought. She forced herself to look back up and stared directly at the pilot, unblinking.

Luli, who was struggling to come up with an answer to a question she never thought would need one, finally said, "For joy, for pleasure. For sadness. To help bring us together. It's the human thing to do." She petered off with, "It fills the quiet moments."

Derain scrutinized the Lieutenant for a long while, "Where the hell were you born not to know that?" He paused sardonically, "Oh, that's right, you weren't. You were made."

Galena glared at the bounty hunter and replied in a staccato fashion, "That's right. Made. Built. Not born. We drones were only taught that which would make us useful tools for the rest of you natural-borns. We have no music, nothing that brings us together. We're not considered human." Everyone pulled back from the vehemence that radiated from her.

Luli waited until the tension in the lounge lessened, "For me, as a cyborg, I play to feel more human. It's one of the few things I can do to reaffirm that I still am."

The rest of the evening went quietly. Luli eventually excused herself to go to the bridge. The jump gate rendezvous would occur in a few hours and she wanted to plan the route to Zangspur. Barney went down to the machine room to build casings for more of his sensors. Anton and Derain both stayed in the lounge, but avoided making eye contact.

Jacquie left to go to her cabin to audit the books. This was purely a cargo run and a legal one at that. The shipping container that Marta, back

Jon Gray Lang

on Chalman's, had secured for her would net a substantial pay off once delivered. It would be nice to stay in the black for a change.

The passenger container was more of a 'just because' delivery. Why run empty on one rack, if you could eke out some of the fuel cost and fill it with a low paying gig? The passengers would be seated in rows in the container for the duration of the trip. They wouldn't be given access to the ship as was standard travel protocol per the Consortium.

That was a rule she was fine and dandy with. Total trip time would be a short twenty seven hours. Just thirteen hours to get out of this system and the remainder in the Spur system. She rubbed her temples and turned back to her data pad to see what cargo runs were currently available on Zangspur.

***

Galena found herself in the cargo bay. She had been given her own small cabin on the ship but after being imprisoned for years, it felt too much like a cell. The cargo bay was the largest room on board and the openness of it helped to calm her nerves. "The walls don't feel as if they are closing in on me. I can breathe."

Luli's voice rang out over the ships comm, "Gate jump in T minus 5."

Galena looked around and slowly

reached for her tags. Free again. Not only free, but part of a team again. She had forgotten how much she missed that. But would these people turn on her? "I don't know," she muttered to the walls.

***

Luli stared through the bow port window at the jump gate. It was constructed as a gigantic circle built out of scaffolding with a ring of wormhole generators bolted at the compass points. There was a station tower with a ship's lock built into it. This was where the crew that ran the gate worked. Every gate had a two ship complement for defense. This particular jump gate had a frigate locked to the tower with a destroyer floating nearby.

She already had relayed their travel destination and ship designation to the tower; the go ahead came shortly after. All that remained was to wait for the generators to power up the gate to create the worm hole. She watched as the four generators sparked up and a whirlpool slowly formed inside the ring. Once the whirlpool had grown to fill the ring, the center became a twirling tempest before it opened into a roiling tube, similar to the eye of a storm.

The Matilda edged forward until the gravity of the newly created worm hole pulled it in. A feeling of disorientation came over the crew as the ship rocketed past the jump gate ring. Once the Matilda materialized an hour later at the other end of their journey, they were given the travel release by the jump gate crew in the Spur system.

"And, we're through," Luli's voice rang over the ships comm. "Trajectory set for Zangspur. Short system. Arrival will be in half a day. We can all take a nap now."

The hours of travel by sublight crawled by. Most of the crew had shuffled off to their bunks. As she lay on the cargo bay decking, Galena noticed a whitish vapor materializing out of the vent system. "Maybe I should go talk to the pilot about this?" She rose up and headed out.

***

Luli registered an incoming transmission on the communications board. She queued it up and the woman on the other end asked for Derain. With a slight shrug, she keyed the comm system over to Derain's cabin and let him know.

Derain thanked her before he set the transmission to private. A female voice came over the comm with a very simple, short message, "Mr. Leon sends his regards." The line dropped. Derain nervously started to look around. He also noticed a strange pale vapor that billowed through the vent system.

Luli's voice came over the comm, "I have a ship, inbound. Arrival in 20 minutes. Ship is not replying to ident request. Captain, prep for boarding?" She waited for a response. There was nothing. "Captain?" She keyed over to Derain's cabin, "Derain, something is setting off sensors in the main shaft. I am not getting a response from the Captain either."

Derain had already donned a breather by this point. He pulled it aside to key the comm, "Some sort of gas is being pumped through the ventilation system. Doesn't smell like death. Maybe a sleeping gas? See if you can shut off the airflow for now. I'll check out the shaft." He brought the mask back up and buckled on his sidearm. As he closed the hatch, he heard Luli's voice, "This approaching ship have anything to do with that private transmission of yours, Derain? Hello?"

Derain quick stepped down to the lift. The lift doors opened and the Lieutenant was splayed out on the floor. He checked for a pulse before he moved inside. "Just knocked out," he whispered to himself. He checked his sidearm and rode down to the second deck. Once the door opened, he dragged the Lieutenant out and propped her against the wall.

As he came up to the hatch of the gym, he looked through the small window, but didn't see any movement on the inside. The interior lights went off as he opened the hatch. Air flow came to a stop as life support was also shut down, "That should curtail someone's plans, at least." He stepped into the gym and side walked toward the main shaft. The shaft hatch lay open and the vapor seemed thickest here.

Jon Gray Lang

***

Luli tried to bring the systems up, but all the power to the bridge had been cut. She pounded on the hatch, but it wouldn't budge.

She muttered under her breath, "Locked in. Not cool."

There was nothing she could do. She watched the other ship sidle up to the Matilda and connect to the top deck airlock. It was definitely a newer craft than the Matilda; bigger, more of a war ship. It had quite the set of visible armaments on it. The Matilda shuddered once the airlocks connected.

***

Derain stepped toward the main shaft and the vapor began to dissipate. As he came up onto the main shaft, he peered in, but didn't see anything. But he did feel the pressure of a barrel as it pressed into his back.

"I'll take that Mr. Tiwi," stated a woman behind him.

Derain handed his pistol over to her. The barrel pressed into his back until he moved forward into the shaft. Once he hit freefall, he felt the woman push him toward the port hatch. The hatch to the passenger container had been blown off its hinges. Two men stepped out into the shaft to collect him and tied his wrists together. Through

Jon Gray Lang

the corner of his eye, he watched another woman push a sleeping Barney down toward him. There were laser torch burns all around the inside of the hatch. A sickly sweet scent wafted out from the open container pod.

When the woman came around to face him, she said, "Thank you for cooperating, Mr. Tiwi." Her weapon slid home as two more men came up behind her. "Would you please tell these gentlemen where we can find the rest of your little band?" She put her hand up to her ear before she said aloud, "Never mind. My compatriots now have them all in custody. Please follow me."

He followed her into the opened container. The other passengers had been slaughtered in their seats. Blood droplets floated in the air within the container due to the lack of gravity. From a far corner, Barney's snores verified that he was sound asleep. Derain watched as a trussed up Jacquie was brought inside, followed by two men who brought in a beaten and bloody Luli. They were unceremoniously dumped in the same corner as Barney. The woman in command turned to face Derain once again.

"Our proposition is simple, Mr. Tiwi. We take one Anton Roane with us and the rest of your group lives. If you do not agree to these terms, we will open this ship to space with you and the rest still onboard." Without waiting for an answer, she continued, "I'm glad we have an understanding." She nodded over to one of the men behind her before cupping her hand to her ear. The man pulled out a pistol and fired directly into Derain's chest. "The pilot was a cyborg? Really? We will have to reinforce the importance of details to our information gatherers." She waved to her team, "We're off this boat."

She led the group to the lift. The two carried a comatose Anton between them. Once on the top deck, they headed to the airlock. Five of her people were laid out in the hallway to the airlock.

"That cyborg was tougher than expected, eh? Those older deep spacer models can be," she mused. "Get those men back on board. We have what we came for."

The rest of her men grabbed the others and brought them through the airlock. The last of her people closed the airlock hatch on the Matilda's side before he headed over to their ship. Once over, he closed the airlock and retracted the tunnel. When he turned around, he noticed that the spacesuits had been tossed randomly about.

He sighed before he began straightening up the area, "Why can't Gary ever hang the suits properly? That guy is going to drive me... uh?" He turned as he saw something out of the corner of his eye.

Someone or something was running toward him in one of their suits. He backed up and tried to get distance from the thing. It moved unnaturally, like an old world marionette from the stories his grandparents had told him. He threw up his arms to block a strike to his head but before he could call out, a second strike took him in the throat, crushing it. He struggled to breathe as the puppet person pulled his knife and stabbed him through the eye.

***

Galena woke to find herself wearing a spacesuit in an airlock of a ship she didn't know. There was a dead man on the deck in front of her. In her hand she held a knife with blood sprayed all over her fist. *'Where am I? What is going on?'* she wondered. She walked over to the airlock window and saw the Matilda as it floated dead in space.

"What's the last thing I remember?" she said out loud. "I was in the cargo bay and started feeling light headed. The last thing I remember is passing out in the lift. Were we pirated?"

She heard voices coming through the open hatch to the airlock. She ran over to the hatch and closed it immediately. For a moment of panic, she stood there before she reached for the controls to the outer hatch.

"Already in a suit for some reason. Might as well take advantage of it." She pulled the handle to release the outer hatch. She latched herself to the guide rod and watched as the recently killed man shot out into space. Once the pressure was equalized, she unlatched herself and headed out to the hull of this unknown vessel. She jammed the knife in her hand into the gap for the hatch, preventing it from being able to close. She scrabbled along the hull until she found a good vantage point of the airlock. She tied herself down and looked out toward the Matilda. It took some fiddling with the comm system built into the suit before she found a wide broadcast channel.

"Luli? Luli, you there?" She waited a minute before she tried again, "Luli? Do you copy?"

fourteen

Life on Mars

Frozen bodies floated around the tumbling derelict ship. Its aft had been blown out and a long rent had been sheared through the port side. As the government ship, designation M33, dragged its spotlights along the torn hull, a dead eyed corpse bounced off the bow port.

"By the Major!" exclaimed the spotlight operator when she flinched from it. "I hate these clean ups." Her light flickered over the ship's designation, "Confirmed. It's the Vogelgesang, sir."

"Still no signs of life, sir," spoke the scanner technician. "Should we send in a search team?"

"Of course you should send in a team. How can we be sure until we have a body?" groused the Captain. He keyed the intercom to the landing crews, "Chief, send three crews. Identify and catalog all on board. Have a team collect and identify all of these floaters, too." His hand waved out toward the detritus orbiting their target. "Pull the ship's records and beam them to us as soon as possible."

"Understood Captain. Chief out." Chief Bull turned to his people, "You heard the man! Three teams, full gear, no atmo. Move, move, move!" He watched in satisfaction as they scurried into their landers already geared up. He addressed the pilots of the smaller craft, "You lot are up on net duties." He pulled on his helmet and boarded the lead lander.

"Mort duties team. Once out, launch and deploy. Let's do this by the numbers, people," stated their Lieutenant over the net ships comm.

As the landers exited the launch bay, the two net ships followed. Once free of their ship, the nets were deployed and the gathering of the bodies started. The three landers hooked onto the corpse of the Vogelgesang at airlock points that still looked intact.

***

On the bridge of the government ship, the Captain paused a moment before he clicked the comm to a private channel, "Doctor, we have located the ship you requested. She has been gutted and there are no life signs. We are currently

Jon Gray Lang

collecting bodies and running ident on the ones we have secured."

A rasping voice came back through the comm channel, "Please keep me informed with your findings, Captain."

"Gives me the creeps that woman does," grumbled the Captain.

"Sir?" asked the scanner technician.

"Keep searching for life. We need to be thorough," replied the Captain.

Hours later, the cargo bay was littered with rows of corpses. Technicians went down each line cataloging faces and prints before they moved onto the next one. The last lander had returned with the final load of cadavers from the derelict.

From the ship's records, an alarm had registered a prison break and the remaining crew had launched via escape pods. The ship had then been attacked by an unknown assailant and everyone left on board had been killed.

They had only found mention of the ship from a report filed by one of the crewman who had escaped. He had turned up dead a week later. Oddly, every single crewman not aboard the ship had been found dead shortly after their landing on the nearby planet Gellert. It was quite obvious that someone was hard at work to erase any trail back to the ship as well as any trail from the Vogelgesang itself.

"But the devil is in the details," muttered the Captain. Some bodies would be missing and this would limit who could be involved. The Doctor was only interested in one person, though; a genorg. Not a high chance that a drone would have survived on board a prison ship. Never mind one opened up to space.

"Captain, we have a full catalog of the dead and the prison ship's manifest. We are missing a total of six, sir," stated the Mortuary Affairs officer.

"Is a Galena Chadov one of them?" asked the Captain.

"Yes sir. The drone that you requested special instructions on remains unaccounted for," replied the officer. "Strangely, all but one of the six was involved in the police action on Tigron. Four were incarcerated as terrorists and the drone was imprisoned for war crimes."

"You should end that speculation, Lieutenant," interrupted the Captain. He keyed the comm to the Doctor's private channel, "We have catalogued all of the bodies. Your drone is definitely one of the missing."

"I knew it, Captain. My prize creation would not be taken so easily. We will find her Captain, we will," said the Doctor. "And when we do," she murmured into the comm, "We can finally see what those beasts put in that little head of yours, my little pet."

Jon Gray Lang

fifteen

Running Home

"Systems coming on line... Scanning for damage... No permanent damage found... Running outlying scan... Three living organisms in close proximity... No movement... Activation of wetware in progress... Loading... Loading..."

Luli woke slowly. It felt like someone had taken a bat to her cranium. Her eyelids fluttered until she was able to focus. She looked around and stared blankly at the scenery. Confusion hit her as she tugged at her wrists, but couldn't separate them.

"Where in the nine hells am I?" she wondered. "Personnel transport container and tied up. Good chance I'm still aboard Matilda."

A voice came over the main comm channel faintly, "Luli? Luli are you there?"

"What's she doing on the comm?"

She saw Derain passed out and floating to the left before she noticed that she was piled up with Jacquie and Barney.

"Luli, do you copy?"

"Need to get these restraints off." She pulled with all her strength to separate her wrists. The bands cut into her skin before they rubbed into her plasteel chassis. The Captain started to blink and mumble once the bands snapped. The pilot's fist went directly into the Captain's face, splitting her lip.

"Ow!" she cried out as she struggled to get away. She calmed a moment before demanding, "Wha was tha for? Wait. Where are we?"

"Luli? Anyone? Is anyone there?"

"What's she doing on the comm?" asked Jacquie. "Last thing I remember I was going over our accounts."

"We were boarded. Full power shut down. Though from the looks of this, it was an inside job," Luli intimated as she indicated all the dead passengers. "Anton is missing and the Lieutenant is on the comm. Things have definitely gone pear shaped. Here, let me help you with your binds."

A muffled voice came from underneath them, "Why is everyone on top of me?"

***

On board the unmarked ship, confusion reigned for a completely different reason.

"What would cause Marcus to space himself? Why would he do that and then jam the bloody hatch?" screamed the woman as she stood in a pile of the bodies of her own men.

"Captain. We're picking up wide spectrum comm signals being broadcast from our hull," replied a voice over the internal comm.

"Cloak us then! Get a team out there and silence it!" the woman yelled.

"Aye, aye."

"At least now I have an answer. More information that would have been useful to have! I am going to teach those data gatherers what it means when someone forgets to get all the valid information on a target. Especially if the missing information is a whole crewman!" screamed the Captain.

The voice over the comm sounded sheepish as it said, "We just lost our communication array, Captain."

She growled as she turned to the men who had brought in the man known as Rabbit, "Get that man stowed below... now."

***

On board the Matilda, Barney had run to the engine room to bring the power back on line. They had been lucky as it had been a cleanly

Jon Gray Lang

done job. "She'll be kicking over soon!" he shouted into the comm.

Luli ran to the lift to get back to the bridge. Jacquie had stayed behind to see if she could wake Derain. It took some doing, but he finally came around, "We've got work to do, so get off your ass."

The pair of them took off for the lift as the interior lights flickered back to life.

"Good work, Barney!" she yelled over her shoulder.

Luli had had to climb up the lift ladder, but by the time Derain and Jacquie had reached it, the lift was operational again. They came through the hatch to see Luli already secured into the pilot's seat.

"Strap in. They're using some kind of cloaking device. I'm tracking them through the comm signal from the Lieutenant."

"The Lieutenant? But she was out when I dragged her out of the lift..." a confused Derain uttered.

"Derain, shut up and bring the weapons systems on line. We can't let them leave," ordered the Captain.

"Aye, aye."

"Luli, has Galena seen Anton? Did they take him?"

"She says she hasn't seen him."

***

Galena looked down at the coil gun in her hand that had come with the suit. She had already destroyed their communications array and blasted at least one man clean off the hull. "This thing sure packs a wallop." She had been edging back toward the engines and the assailants had been eager to pursue her into a corner. "But that's what I wanted anyway," she smirked.

She holstered the coil gun and pulled out the knife strapped to the suit when she saw movement out to her far left. "This suit sure does come equipped with what you need." She crept toward the last position where she had observed movement. As the helmet crested over the obstruction on the hull, she released her mag boots and accelerated toward him. She slammed into him hard, but his boots held. With a deft flick of the wrist, she quickly cut his airline and re-anchored herself. She watched as he asphyxiated while clawing at the cut airline until he no longer struggled. She sheathed the knife and pulled the coil gun free. She deactivated his boots and drag-floated the body toward the nearest engine. She glanced over her shoulder and fired at the only movement she saw. She pulled the dead man's suit retrieval board and activated the beacon. With his mag boots reactivated, she sent him sailing toward the engine.

"The target is the homing beacon, copy?" she said over the channel.

Jon Gray Lang

***

"Captain, we have a homing beacon deployed off our port engine," the first mate reported.

"How the hell did that happen?"

Just then, the ship shook from an impact.

"We, uh just lost the port engine!"

"Prepare for boarding. All hands!" she cried into the comm.

***

"I believe that was a direct hit. Good job Derain. But fire again to be sure," ordered Jacquie.

***

Anton woke to the wail of sirens and found himself in what appeared to be a small cell. "What have I gone and done now?" he wondered out loud.

"Prepare for boarding. All hands!" rang out from the comm.

Anton tottered to his feet as the entire ship lurched from an impact. He grabbed for one of the walls and skidded toward the only hatch. Two men, who may have been his guards, ran down the hall and around a corner. He hummed to

Jon Gray Lang

himself as he looked at the lock and grunted in surprise.

"Seriously? An r9DP-j? I didn't think people still used these things."

He pulled a thin sliver of plastic out of the lining of his boot and placed it over the locking mechanism. He dragged his finger over the plastic in a series of patterns. Satisfied, he pulled the plastic sliver off and slid it back into the boot lining. With a quick turn of the handle, he strutted out past the hatch.

"Now if I were aboard a ship that was under attack from my friends, where could I be the biggest pain in the ass?"

***

Galena was hard pressed on the hull of the marauder. One of the engines was knocked out and the ship had started to spin. Luckily, their pilot had killed the other main engine so the spin wasn't increasing exponentially.

She was down to a couple shots. That was all that was left in the last coil gun she scavenged off a corpse that had still been magnetically attached to the hull. There were still at least five or six people after her, and she had lost track of two of them. She glanced over at the Matilda as it came closer, still locked on to her comm signal.

Jon Gray Lang

***

Anton peeked around a corner and spied an open hatch to the engineering room. He strolled in as if he belonged, but the room was unoccupied. As he looked around, he noticed a large box with wires trailing from it. The label stamped to the side read, Plasma Cloak Generator. He happily yanked out handfuls of wiring.

***

Luli was completely focused on the comm signal that beamed from Galena that she nearly freaked out when the other ship appeared and immediately filled the bow port. "Whoa! Cloak is down! Pulling back to meet its spin!" Luli cried out.

***

"The cloak just dropped, Captain. It's gone offline!" cried the Scanner Technician First Class.

The Captain screamed, "How is this happening?" She had never had such a fiasco happen under her command.

"The Matilda is meeting our spin, Captain."

She took a moment to calm herself. How did this all go wrong? There were only four of them on board. They had the fifth member locked up below. She had at least four-to-one odds. She keyed the comm, "Hull teams, have you taken care of our problem?"

"We are still engaged, Captain. We have the adversary pinned down. It should be eradicated soon," came the reply.

"Keep me updated, Corporal." She keyed the comm off.

***

Anton yanked a comm device off one of the fellows who had attempted to interrupt his activities. He pulled off the back and adjusted some of the internal wiring. "Anton to Matilda. You there, Matilda?"

Luli's voice came back over the channel, "Anton, did you get free?"

"Of course! Did you think some simple lock would keep me out? Now a stint in solitary, that's a different story," he replied jovially.

"Anton, this is Jacquie. Do you think you can open the airlocks from where you are?"

He looked around, "Possibly. I might need to change locations. How soon?"

"I'm thinking of a Red Mary. Can you do it?"

He took a moment before he answered querulously, "I believe so. Do you think it's that necessary?"

"I do."

"Give me the signal and enough time to lockdown. Anton, out," he stated before he tore into the engineering panel.

***

Luli looked over at Jacquie, "I've checked with the Lieutenant. She doesn't think she can hold out much longer. We sure we want to do this?"

"What's a Red Mary?" asked Derain.

Jacquie ignored Derain's question, "I don't want to, but there are too many of them. I don't know what else we can do." She turned back to the comm, "Barney, start setting up a stationary jump. We're doing a Red Mary."

"I think I'm going to be sick," came his reply.

"Spins are equalized. Engaging the tunnel," stated Derain.

"Anton, give me the ready signal," Jacquie requested over the comm.

***

Anton attached the helmet he finished pulling off of the previous wearer to his suit and hurried back to engineering. He locked down the hatch and gave the ready signal to the Matilda.

***

Galena was surrounded and pinned down with nowhere else to move. She saw the Matilda's tunnel connect to the ship she was anchored to and lock into place. It was at this moment that everything... went... wrong...

The Matilda stretched, then folded into itself and dragged the ship she was attached to along with her. Everything disgorged back out, but seemed backwards... reversed. Space was no longer black; it was dark, but lit with indescribable colors as if from a vast distance. What felt like a mist enveloped her and the smell of it somehow came through her suit's filters and it stank. She almost threw up. The people who surrounded her didn't fare much better. She felt the vessel beneath her shudder and watched atmosphere get jettisoned out into the light fog of this environment... this place. It was eerily quiet and different from what she was used to; almost pregnant with some dark promise.

Suddenly black shapes, like beasts from nightmares, fell toward the two ships and tried to rip into the hulls. She hunkered down and watched as these things... nothing seemed to quantify what they were... ripped the people who surrounded her to shreds. The monsters poured through the open airlocks and she tried to tune out the screams of the others that came in fits and bursts through her suit's channels. Something about the beasts felt somehow familiar, as if she had seen them before.

Jon Gray Lang

A powerful pull came from the Matilda that caused her to look over. She felt turned inside out as the Matilda folded into itself and dragged this craft in with it. The two ships then folded back into normal space. At this point, she vomited in her helmet.

***

Luli's voice came over the comm, "God, I hate that. Worst engine ever! Why would someone build such a horrible contraption? Okay everybody, the Captain requests a sound off from those off ship."

***

Galena heard Anton's voice count off. She struggled a moment, then managed to count off herself. He lived! Somehow, he had survived and was somewhere on board this hulk. She stood up and looked around as bits and pieces of what had once been her adversaries fluttered in space. She maneuvered over to the nearest open airlock and stepped inside the marauder. It was worse than what she had seen outside. Humans ripped apart and thrown haphazardly around. Hatches torn open; their disgorged contents littering the hallway. She stumbled aimlessly through the ship until she ran into Barney.

"I've got the Lieutenant," Barney

announced over the comm.

"Bridge hatch still locked. No living crew so far," came Derain's voice in reply over the comm.

"Found Anton and closing the locks. Meet up at the bridge, people," ordered the Captain.

The crew of the Matilda stood ready at the bridge hatch. The ship had partial gravity working in sections, but it was absent up here. Barney worked a blowtorch over the lock that eventually sparked before it popped. Jacquie and Anton took up positions straight on, while Derain and Galena took up positions to the sides of the hatch. Barney tugged on the handle until the seal separated. The hatch slowly swung open onto madness. Derain recognized the woman who had ordered him shot. Her lifeless, mangled body floated past, mingled amongst the shell casings fired from her old handgun. Another body was partially stuck through the broken bow port. But what drew all their attention most was the wormlike thing that disintegrated before their very eyes.

"What the hell is that?" Derain hissed.

"I... I didn't think they could come through," stammered Jacquie.

Barney started shaking, "This is beyond bad. We need to get out of here."

Galena walked over to it. "They can't live here... Not for long anyway." She turned to see that everyone had shied away from her. "We're safe. Safe from them here." Her hands dropped to her sides.

    "At a later date, you'll have to let us know how you know that," muttered the Captain. She ignored the Lieutenant's shrug and continued, "Luli, see what we can scavenge from this boat. Anton and Derain; empty out the armory and the food stores. Barney, see if we can grab that cloaking device. Uh, Ms. Chadov, could you assist Barney? I'll pull the log books."

***

    Later that solar day, the crew met up in the lounge on board the Matilda. Luli had already re-plotted their course to Zangspur. The food and medical supplies retrieved from the dead ship had left them in the flush. The weapons stores had mostly been on the illegal end of things, especially in the Spur system. Luli actually had found some system charts that she didn't already have. The log books had proven to be empty copies and lacked a registration guide. It had taken the whole crew to drag the cloaking device back to the Matilda. Barney wasn't certain he could get it to work, but it never hurt to try.

    Barney continued his breakdown, "No damage to the Matilda except for the destroyed hatch to the passenger container off the main shaft. We've bagged the bodies and put them in the hangar bay for keeping. It's going to take me some time to replace that hatch."

Jon Gray Lang

"We'll have a nice stay over on Zangspur until that gets repaired," noted the Captain.

"What are we going to do with the passenger container?" asked Luli.

"It's going to have to stay bolted on until the hatch is repaired." Barney thought for a moment, *'Not sure how we're going to explain away the bodies.'*

"I've already sent out a piracy attack warning. We'll be hassled at port by the local merc police." Jacquie growled a bit before she continued, "Leave the ship as is. The repairs will be completed after the investigation."

Luli leaned over and whispered into the Captain's ear. Jacquie's face grew tight as she continued, "We'll have to figure out what to do with you Anton, since everyone seems to be after you." She jeered, "Only you can somehow create trouble when you've been in lockdown for years." She paid no heed to his rebuttal, "Derain? I need to talk to you now."

"I want to talk to you too," Derain replied. "Can you explain to me what the bloody hell just happened?"

"I'll cover it."

Galena followed Derain and the Captain as they chose a table far away from everyone else. She sat down just within hearing distance of their conversation.

"Luli tells me you received a

communication just as that ship came into scanner range. You mind telling me what it was about?" She clenched her hands tightly, "More importantly, were you expecting something and not going to tell me? If so, we need to revisit our business relationship as of right now. Meaning you're off this boat once we get dirt side."

Derain looked shocked before his face smoothed over. "I did receive a communication right as that ship came into view and no, I did not expect anything." He looked directly at her, "You mind telling me why someone would want your friend in there that bad? That is quite an elaborate set up to grab one man. And what the goona is a Red Mary?"

Jacquie was silent a moment before she made up her mind, "Okay. I didn't think you'd roll on us, but I had to be sure." She exhaled as her eyes looked up to the ceiling, as old painful memories flashed to the fore. "What we call a Red Mary is exactly what you saw; what we just did. We pull a ship that is open to space into wherever that hellish mechanism takes us and let those... creatures finish it off. It's a last resort sort of action and both times we've done it, I've been afraid that they'd get us too."

"The second time? You've only done this once before?"

She hesitated for a moment, but as the pain of the memories poured from her, she dove into the tale, "The first time, we didn't even know what would happen. It just seemed better than the alternative."

Neither of them noticed Galena, who had leaned in a bit to overhear better.

Jacquie paused as she collected her thoughts, "You know I grew up on this ship, right? To be more accurate, I was born on her. It used to just be my mom, dad, Barney and me; that's it. We had some lean years and some abundant years, but it was always enough to get by. We'd even had dealings with pirates, but we'd never been boarded. Not until the worst night of my life."

"They'd caught us unaware and boarded us while I was asleep. My father had been the only one awake. They slit his throat from ear to ear before he could raise a warning. My mother's screams were what woke me. I scrambled out of bed and made it down to the machine room before they started tearing our cabins apart. I hid in an old smuggling compartment and hoped no one would find it. When my mother's screams stopped I just cried. I cried myself to sleep."

"I woke up, and by chance, they hadn't found me. I didn't know how long I had been out. I didn't even know if Barney was still alive. I worked up my courage to try to find him; to help him, if I could. I mean, he was the only other person I knew. The first thing I came across was my mother's body in the cargo bay. Her lifeless eyes stared at nothing. A little bit further back, my father's body had been thrown onto the decking. It was hard to keep from bawling right there, so I ran out of the bay through the airlock and into the pirate ship."

"We had picked up a special delivery of whiskey at our last port and the pirates had discovered it. I had to step around and over a lot of the ones who had passed out. But I wasn't able to find Barney anywhere. Worried, I finally worked up my nerve to go deeper into the pirate ship."

"It wasn't much bigger than the Matilda, but it had a huge crew. I wandered through that ship skirting past men and women singing, fighting and sleeping off their drunk. It took me a long time before I came across some men beaten half to death as a sort of trail to Barney. They had locked him in a cage. He was black and blue and out cold. That's also where I first met Anton."

"He was on that ship? As a pirate?" queried Derain.

"No. Not as a pirate, but as another prisoner. He saw me and pleaded with me to help him escape. I asked him what had happened to Barney and he told me how the pirates had come in antagonizing him until he fought them off. They eventually pinned him down and kept hitting and kicking him until he stopped moving. Rabbit was close enough to my age and in a bad spot, so I decided to trust him. Who else did I have? Plus, Barney is pretty heavy for his size and there was no way I was getting him out of there by myself. It took a while to get Barney back on board the

Matilda, but we finally succeeded. Every time we passed one of the sleeping raiders, Anton would slide the blade of a small knife into their temple."

"His handiwork didn't go unnoticed, though. By the time we got to the lift on the Matilda, we could hear curses and shouted orders echoing through the airlock tunnel. Luckily, Barney woke as we were hustling him onto the lift. He was the one who told us to head for the engine room. It had two of the strongest hatches inside the ship and a single entry point. Right after we got off the lift, it immediately went back down. We ran through the hatch to the gym and locked it. We locked the hatch at one end of the main shaft just as an arc lighter began cutting through the gym hatch. We rushed to the engine room and locked that hatch behind us, too. They knew where we were and we had nowhere else to run."

Galena leaned in as the story started to pick up pace.

"We watched them cut through the hatch at the far end of the main shaft. It looked like the entire crew of that ship wanted to rip us completely apart. Rabbit was huddled in the corner whispering, "Not again" over and over. Barney was scrabbling for any idea that could get us out of this. But me? I just froze, staring dumbly as those pirates marched down to the last hatch between us and began to cut it open."

At this point, Galena had fallen out of her chair and both Derain and Jacquie turned in her direction. She nonchalantly stood up, brushed herself off, sat down again and pointedly looked away.

Jacquie waited a moment before she jumped back into her story. "As the hatch started to glow red, I stepped back. Barney yelled out, "Here goes nothing" and tripped a lever he had wired to that weird machine back there. We didn't know what would happen or what it could do. Barney had surmised over the years that it was some sort of engine, but he didn't know what kind. He had been compiling data on it for decades by then, but no one had ever come across anything like it. Anyway, the ship jumped to whatever hellish plane it goes to and those things came in through a damaged airlock on the pirate ship. I watched through that port window in the hatch that was still warm to the touch as all those people we're eaten or absorbed by those things. I felt elation for surviving the pirates and horror that we were going to die the same way."

"How old were you?"

"I was fifteen."

Derain thought back and shivered. After a moment he asked, "But why call it Red Mary? I still don't understand."

"My mother's name was Mary." Jacquie shook herself before she changed subjects, "Getting back to today, who sent the communication? Can you tell me that at least?"

Anger tinged Derain's words as he responded, "It was a woman claiming to work for

Mr. Leon. I don't know if that's true or just another part of their ruse. But if it is true, your friend in there has powerful enemies." He paused a moment before he continued, "I'm going to see what I can find out about who might be after him and how much of a threat he poses to the safety of this crew. But you better confront Anton and see what he's hiding. It's been at least five years since you last saw the man regularly. He might not be that same kid you remember." Derain stood up and left Jacquie to sit alone at the table.

sixteen

Fly Me to the Moon

As the Matilda made her approach to Zangspur, Galena thought back on the story Jacquie had told. It was so unlike her own upbringing that it seemed incredibly alien. She and her many sisters, all genetically identical, were kept in pods for what felt like many years. They only saw each other in passing every day as they went from one menial instruction course to another. Galena hadn't known that the tasks they received instruction in were the jobs the natural-borns refused to do. She learned this and many other lessons from the natural-borns when she had first been released on work duty to a mine. As she had gotten older, she had figured out that it had only been twelve years before she had been sold to the mine. It was the age that all drones were initially purchased.

Jon Gray Lang

She had been fortunate, though. She had seen some of her sisters crushed in tunnel collapses, but had survived herself to live another day. The mine had run dry after her fourth year there. She was sold again as collateral to cover the financial loss of the mine to a factory. In many ways, the factory was much more like her upbringing. She got to live in an almost pod like environment with others of her sisters. It was simple work and the hours were long. She learned more lessons of the life of a drone in this environment. Drones like her generally had very short life spans due to the dangerous kind of work that they were used for.

Eventually, she was sold again before the military purchased her contract outright; before the trial, prison and here. She had served as a menial laborer in a planetary government house. It was strange to be among natural-borns, especially as she did not seem to exist to them. The work consisted mostly of ferrying messages to and from the various political groups in their wheeling's and dealing's. She learned later that drones were bought for this function due to the fact that they couldn't read or write and because they were beneath notice. Her time in this field had been short as someone in the military had purchased her contract due to her work history. It took years of intensive training to turn her into a 'real person' at least as far the Consortium was concerned. She was put on duty; duty which led to her arrest, imprisonment and eventual rescue aboard this ship. By comparison, the Captain's life seemed utterly alien.

***

As Luli waited for clearance, she wondered how long they would be delayed in port. If things went smoothly, they might get salvage rights to the ship that had attacked them. This was pretty unlikely, though. That's why the Captain had ordered the snatch-n-grab of the most valuable goods on the dead raider. Barney had gone over the cloaking device they had pulled and thought it could be integrated into the Matilda. Its power requirements were high, but with some adjustments, it should work. It had taken them a while to pull all six emitters off the outer hull. These had quickly been attached to the hull of the Matilda prior to their voyage planet side.

Jacquie had expedited the drop for the cargo container and Luli brought the Matilda in for a solid landing. There was no record of the passenger container on file at Zangspur, but the local mercenaries, who were employed as the local police force, waited to get on board to start their investigation. All the illegal salvage they had pulled had been 'hidden in plain sight' for the port inspection and homicide investigation.

Anton, on the other hand, would remain hidden within the walls of the ship until the Matilda was no longer listed as evidence. His stay between the outer wall and the wall to the sickbay would not be a pleasant one. It was an old maintenance shaft for the landing gear and it was just wide and long enough to pace in. There wasn't room for much else. Anton explained that he didn't know why a Mr. Leon was after him, but they put him in hiding for his safety.

Jacquie had left the conversation unsatisfied with his answers and that bounty hunter fellow decreed he would look for the answers that Anton wouldn't voice. Even Luli was unhappy with his lack of an answer. But he just didn't know. Barney pointed out that he had plenty of time to think about the whys and what ifs now. There wouldn't be much else to do back there, anyway.

After the first of many examinations by the local investigative force, they were given permission to go planet side. Since they didn't know when they would be able to leave Zangspur, the search for new cargo was put on hold. Derain had left the ship to look into some local bounty jobs to bide the time. Barney was fully invested in the hatch repair job in the main shaft. If he got it done with time to spare, he still had the cloaking device to play with. This left Luli, Jacquie and their new crewmember, Galena, with a lot of free time.

***

Jacquie looked over at Galena who sat at one of the tables in the ship's lounge. Luli had lent her a data pad and she was busy going through the recorded history of the last three years. Zangspur was relatively liberal when it came to media access, but as was always the case, not everything was shared with the populace.

The Captain stood up, walked over to Galena and announced, "I think I promised you a shopping trip. You are sorely under equipped and we need you set up with your own gear." Luli stepped into the lounge, "Luli, you up for going out?"

"What and leave Barney here to fend for himself? Never!" Luli bounced over and snatched her data pad out of Galena's hands. "How could I possibly leave him to such a boring fate?" She looked pointedly at Galena before she headed for the lounge hatch, "Are you coming, Lieutenant?"

"Now?" asked Galena.

The Captain followed Luli out, "No time like the present, right?"

Galena stood quickly with a flustered look on her face, "Okay." She checked her pockets to find them empty, "Let me grab a few things..."

"We'll meet you in the cargo bay. Let's go Luli!"

Galena heard a muted 'way ahead of you' as she dashed for the cabin deck and her bunk. She tried to remember where she had put the currency that the Captain had given her. She could just barely hear Jacquie and Luli laugh at something as she discovered it in a drawer. She shoved the mazuma stack into her pocket, shot out the hatch and ran to the lift. When she got down to the bay, the Captain waved them out the main bay doors.

"We're walking?" asked Galena.

"Everything is on lockdown including the Folly until they're done rummaging through my ship. Which means, we walk," Jacquie explained as she headed out onto the tarmac.

Luli shrugged at Galena and followed her out. Galena stood there with a bewildered look before she shot out after the two of them. She listened as Luli and Jacquie traded quips with each other and with other travelers on their stroll through the port district. She finally relaxed and marveled at the various types of ships that were in the port. She listened as her companions talked about the models and who owned or captained them. She was amazed that both women knew so much about all these different craft, but then realized her knowledge of handheld weaponry probably surpassed the knowledge of the two women combined. It gave her something to think about and she used that time to learn as much as she could surreptitiously.

It didn't take terribly long to get to the spacer's market off the port and its menagerie of goods and acquaintances. Jacquie and Luli seemed to know just about everyone as they were stopped by almost every booth keep or passersby. Galena finally realized that Jacquie had been asking around for the best quality goods and lowest prices relevant to her needs. This surprised her. As she took in that information, she noticed that the

Captain looked perturbed from her last conversation. She gave Luli a small nod. In irritation, Luli sighed as her face blanked. The trio headed toward the outskirts of the market nearest the local city.

"What's wrong?" Galena asked the now silent Luli.

Luli gave her an appraising look, "We'll be dealing with some locals and they have particular ideas about people like me. It's going to be a fun day," she lamented.

"People like you?"

"Jacquie? I'm thinking we go for a drink after we get the necessities done," Luli said.

"That sounds like an excellent plan. Well, let's get this over with."

The shops and booths had become less colorful, with more of a monochromatic decorative palette. Eventually they came around a corner to a small shop that had shelves loaded with various electronics and gear for the average spacer. The people who ran the shop seemed rather well to do considering the location, but the other clientele in the shop were dressed in the more monochromatic style of the locals. Galena headed straight over to the shelves that held the different data pad options and Luli followed behind her. She told Galena what she thought would be the best model as a clerk approached Jacquie.

"Excuse me. But that thing must leave now," the store clerk ordered while she pointed at Luli. "We don't serve automatons or their ilk here on Zangspur. You can tell it to go to one of the foreigner's stores; maybe they'll serve its needs."

Another clerk came up to the Captain and said sweetly, "We are, however, quite willing to work with you, madam. That is, if you are fully human?"

The Captain bit back a retort as Luli said loudly, "I'll meet you back outside, Captain." She whispered into Galena's ear, "Just play along, alright?"

Luli sauntered out the door as Galena tried to understand what was going on. Play along? Play along with what? And wasn't Luli a natural-born? Why did they treat her as if she was less than that... as if she were a drone? She was about to ask these questions when she felt the Captain's finger pressed to her lips. She looked at Jacquie quizzically.

"That would be wonderful. And yes, I am fully human, born and bred." She laughed lightly as she dropped her finger from the Lieutenant's mouth, "I am looking to outfit my recently purchased drone, here. She is quite old and so poorly outfitted that it almost seems offensive to bring her into public." Jacquie looked around, "Do you think you can help me rectify this social tragedy?"

"Oh! Of course, madam! We will be quite delighted to assist you in your endeavor," exclaimed the closer of the two clerks.

After a lengthy trip around the small

shop, the Captain led a weighed-down-with-packages Galena back out the door. They met up with Luli and headed back toward the center of the market. They stopped next to a bin where Galena opened her packages and placed the items the Captain had purchased for her all over her person. Drones were not expected to carry currency here; the Captain had informed her on the way out. She deposited the containers directly into the bin.

"That's much easier," she exhaled in relief, "What do we do now?"

"Now we can relax and get you the rest of what you need from people who are not narrowed minded pala naio," spat Luli.

"Strange isn't it that the most bigoted people always seem to live on the main worlds. You'd think it would be the other way around," Jacquie remarked.

"Those people exist everywhere," muttered the Lieutenant.

"Even on board the ship you serve. Look at us calling the kettle black," acknowledged the Captain. "Touché, Lieutenant." Jacquie looked around and spied a tavern. "With that, I owe you a drink and I already owe Luli one as well. Follow me!"

All three women headed toward a small table outside on the porch of the establishment and Jacquie ordered a round of drinks. She decided it was time to get to know this Lieutenant and put her at ease. She had quite a well known military history and yet she was still a complete enigma.

Well into their third round, Barney's voice came over the personal comm channel, "Eh, Jacquie, you there? Those investigative clowns have gone and taken that passenger container as evidence. I've had to run a plasteel patch over the blown hatch to keep the bugs out!"

Jacquie hushed the two ladies and giggled. "You need us back, Barney?"

"No, just letting you know and venting. Barney out."

"Now that, my friends, is an unhappy engineer. I'm ordering us a round to drink in his honor!" Luli shouted as she stood up.

Galena felt pretty flushed. She had never had much of an opportunity to imbibe in her previous careers and there wasn't anything like it in the prison. She felt very relaxed and was enjoying this moment with the Captain... no, with Jacquie and Luli. Luli had told some stories about some of her early career flights and they had all laughed together. Luli returned with a tray of glasses and set down all nine of the increasingly dark drinks.

Galena looked on in shock. "Nine? So many!"

"They're not all for you, silly. Okay Captain, are you ready? We've got to initiate this young lady into the crew! Galena, we slam the first one, savor the second one and sip the last one. One, two, three, go!" she shouted.

Galena hadn't noticed but it had gotten dark out and the market had come alive in lights... lights all around and in many colors. She tried to keep pace with her crew mates, but was steadily having trouble staying focused. As the evening wore on, she lost track of where they were and even what they were doing. At one place they stopped, she felt the heavy beat of a bass system and watched in astonishment as Jacquie and Luli moved to the music. She had never seen anything like it before in her life. Luli brought her another drink and dragged her out onto the floor.

"Dance, girl! Dance!" she cried.

Jacquie tugged her over and put her hands on Galena's hips, "Sway! To the music!"

Galena tried to understand what the two were talking about. She chugged the latest drink that had been shoved into her hands and did her best to feel the beat. She heard laughter and felt embarrassed. Just as her shoulders slumped she felt the Captain's hands on her hips again.

Luli stood in front of her and yelled over her shoulder, "Grab my hips and follow my moves!"

Galena hesitantly put her hands on the pilot's hips and felt the rigid coolness of plasteel on her palms. The hips were gesticulating wildly when she felt them slow down.

"Just follow along!" cried the Captain.

'*What the hell,*' thought Galena. She tried to match the movements of Luli in front of her and the pulls from Jacquie behind her. She paid attention to the way the movements were timed with the beats of the music. She started to relax and just flow with the sound that was all around her. She heard Jacquie and Luli laughing and caught herself laughing along. As she danced she started to feel dizzy. When she stopped dancing though, the world kept on spinning. She heard an "uh oh" off to the side and scrabbled to keep the floor from falling into her.

"I think we need to get her out of here, before she... oh well..." Jacquie said.

"I'll get a towel... uh, a mop." Luli took off.

Galena emptied herself of just about everything she had ingested that day. She felt arms pick her up and carry her back over to the table. From the corner of her eye she saw a blurry Luli clean up something before she tossed some mazuma to one of the staff. Supported between Jacquie and Luli, Galena struggled to stay upright as they headed back to the Matilda and, she hoped, to a bed or decking or something... something to lie on... that didn't move... or spin...

seventeen

Spin, Spin, Sugar

A small lander lit upon the surface of the moon known as Caleb. Two people stepped out of the craft and lightly bounded over to the only thing on the surface that didn't belong. They picked up a badly mangled body and bounded back to the lander. The lander's gear went up, leapt off the moon's surface and shot toward the unmarked hull of the vessel that circled above.

The Chief's voice came over the comm to the Captain, "The body has been identified as a Doctor Saric, the missing crew member of the Vogelgesang. Looks like he's been dead a while and his head is missing. From what the technician tells me, the body has been on this moon for a few days, sir."

"Thank you Chief. Get your people

Jon Gray Lang

back on board." The Captain turned to the communications officer, "Check this system for any news that might give us a lead."

"Yes sir," replied the communications officer. "The only report that comes up is from Chalman's world. A wrecked airship with a deceased pilot has been found on the outskirts of town. Five more unidentified bodies were found a short distance away."

The Captain deliberated a moment, "The only inhabited planet in the system and there just happens to be a pile of bodies? I'd say we have our lead." He looked perturbed as he muttered, "What kind of a monster are we chasing?" He closed his eyes and ordered, "Set a course for Chalman's world, Lieutenant."

***

The Doctor mused over some notes from one of her previous experiments when she received a call from the Captain "The infamous Doctor Saric had been found, dead on the moon."

"Not surprising. The man had always been a fool," the Doctor retorted.

Apparently a pile of bodies had been located on the nearest planet too. "Aah, my pet. You are a work of wonder, my finest achievement. A true destroyer." Pride and excitement hit her as they got closer to her quarry, "Soon you will be with me again," she cackled. "Soon."

eighteen

Danse Russe

Galena woke to find herself in her bunk on board the Matilda. Her clothes were missing and she had no memory of how she had gotten back to the ship. She tried standing, but almost fell over from the pounding in her skull. She fell back on her bunk and clutched her head. It felt as if her skull was too tight for her brain and her eyes wanted to pop out. She turned slowly to see Luli looking down at her with a quirky grin on her face.

"You should let people know if you've never been drinking, miss ma'am. It would make for a cleaner night out." Luli tossed some clothes to her, "And speaking of cleaner, I washed your clothes."

Galena caught the clothes numbly

while she stared blankly at the pilot.

"I brought you these too." She walked into the cabin holding a glass of liquid and two small pills, "These will help with the pain and the queasiness." She waited until Galena had choked them down before she sat alongside her, "Anything else you need?"

"What is happening to me?" Galena asked lamely.

"You are coming down from a fun night out and suffering from making that choice. It's an evil price we all pay at some time. For you, it is now!" Luli patted Galena on the back, "Those pills will get you to a working normal in a little while. The Captain says to take it easy today. Of course, there isn't much else to do as we're still stuck in port."

Galena breathed in slowly before she insisted, "I've never seen or done anything like last night."

"We could tell. Jacquie and I both agree that to be part of this crew, you are going to have to learn to dance." Luli held her hand over her heart, "I have solemnly sworn an oath of the deepest kind to help you make this happen. Do you accept this challenge, Lieutenant Galena Chadov?"

Galena looked blankly at Luli for a moment. She straightened her posture and held her hand over her heart. Her face took on a serious cast, "I do so solemnly swear to learn the skills needed for me to remain a member of this crew."

Jon Gray Lang

Luli laughed lightly which confused Galena. Her hand dropped to her lap and her shoulders slumped. Why was her vow laughable? These people were so strange.

"So serious! I was kidding. You don't need to learn to dance; I just want to teach you. You're already a crew member and that's not going to change unless you want it to. Oh! We'll be heading back into town to finish up your purchasing needs around lunch time, alright?" Luli bantered as she stood up to leave.

"Wait. I don't understand. I'm not used to being treated this way."

"What? Like a person? Well, get used to it."

"May I ask you a question?" asked Galena.

Luli gazed at her a moment then sat back down, "Of course. You can ask me anything. Doesn't mean I'll answer."

She looked searchingly into Luli's eyes, "I overheard the Captain talking about how she met Rabbit and her upbringing before that. I know I shouldn't have been listening, but it was unlike anything I had ever heard. My life, my upbringing has been completely different, even down to last night. But, it has made me wonder about the rest of you." She turned to stare at Luli once again, "How did you end up here, on this ship?"

"That's what you want to know? Sure, it's not a terribly exciting story, but I can do that for you." Luli relaxed and appeared to think back, "Let's see. I had just finished a stint on a small tub of a ship, pulling big cargo ships into dock off the planet Innocent in the Benedictus system. I had landed my last colony ship from the Sol system a year back and was having trouble finding work. I had to rely on my old tug ship skills. Who would've thought that those would be the valuable skills I'd need to feed myself hundreds of years into the future?"

"Wait! You know where the Earth is?"

"Born and bred in the Sol system's asteroid belt. I am one of the last few to know the way back to where it was. And I do mean was. It's gone now, not even the stars shine in that black spot in the curtain of the sky.

"I always thought the Earth was a myth," whispered Galena.

"No myth, I've seen it myself. Just a blue dot in the night sky, but I've seen it. Anyway, after docking that old colony ship, I got work as a tug pilot. I did some gigs in the spacer bars and down on the planet, but it got to a point that I just needed a change of scenery. I figured I'd look for work as a pilot on some of the privately owned merchant class craft. To my surprise, I was highly sought after. Had I known to look there first, who knows where I'd be now, right? Anyway, I felt confident that I could be pretty picky. Every few days, I'd go down to the ship yard and check out the boats and see which one really grabbed me. But, none of them did."

"It was after one of those interviews, that I first saw the Matilda. She was pretty beat up at the time, but she sang to me. I stopped and stared at her when the cargo bay doors opened and out stepped this young girl. A young man came up behind her and then this diminutive older fellow brought up the rear. They all looked as beaten as their ship, but they had a defiance about them. They seemed ready for business and yet completely lost at the same time."

"I didn't even bother with the pleasantries. I just walked right up and asked for a job. We haggled a bit; I gave them some references and was hired the next day. It took a while to get my set up built into her, but Barney knew that ship inside and out. I took her out for the first time a week later and I've been her pilot ever since."

"I wasn't asked for references," murmured Galena.

"Hey, you proved your worth on the job. Anyway, I'm off to the lounge for some food, then the Captain and I will be heading out. You can join us if you want or hang out here. If you come out with us, we promise to be nicer to you. Scouts honor," Luli winked as she headed out.

Galena sat there and absorbed Luli's story when she heard a sudden tapping come from the decking below her. "Is someone there?"

"Hey, Lieutenant, it's me Rabbit. I

overheard you are going back into town. I was wondering if you might pick up some stuff for me."

"I'm not really sure. I'll..."

"I'd really appreciate it if you would get me these things. None of it sends out a signal, if that's what you're worried about," he pleaded.

"Well, it's not that..."

"Excellent, thanks! I really appreciate this! I already stuffed the list in your vent."

Galena groaned as she kneeled on the deck and looked around for the vent. As she pulled a paper list out of the vent, he spoke up again.

"Lieutenant? One more thing, could I borrow enough to cover the cost of that stuff? I'll pay you back as soon as I can. Thanks again!"

Galena heard shuffling sounds recede into the distance as she opened the piece of paper. "Where did he get paper?" She was going to have to explore this boat further at some point. Looking over the paper, she recognized what was listed, "These are weapon parts!"

She stood up, deciding she would go to town to get the rest of her gear taken care of. For the second time in her life, she would be spending her own mazuma. For the first time in her life, someone had borrowed it.

Barney watched as the three ladies left the cargo bay on another adventure into town. It was good to see Jacquie smiling again. She had grown pretty dour in the past year. Not even Luli had been able to pull her out of her funk. She'd had a pretty big grin on this morning, though. It set his heart at ease. Maybe the Lieutenant was exactly what the Captain needed.

nineteen

Jimmy, Jimmy

The Captain of the M33 glanced out the window as he sat beside the Doctor in the crawler. They were on their way to the crash site of the air ship on Chalman's world. The Mortuary Affairs Officer had already taken charge of the seven corpses the local police had in their morgue. The police had been quite happy to get rid of them as the bodies were already designated for the incinerator. He still was taken aback by the idea of burning perfectly good protein. Nothing was wasted on his home world; nothing at all.

The Doctor had requested to come out to the crash site as well as to the site where the other bodies had been retrieved. Every bread crumb, or corpse in this case, on the trail of her creature seemed to excite the Doctor more and more. The Captain had never seen the woman so agitated and he wished he still hadn't. It was off putting to say the least.

From what he had heard, the Doctor's experiment had proven successful years ago and the Consortium wanted more of these trained drones to bring the recently discovered border system into the fold. It had been difficult to keep the system expansion under wraps, but using the drones made it quite easy. Simply because no one cared.

After a few batch failures, the Doctor had sworn that she needed her first test subject, this Galena Chadov, to repeat the process exactly. Her plan to speed up the process was to map its personality over existing drone stock. As far as the Consortium leadership had been concerned, the overhead cost would be limited to equipment and transport. The existing overstock of old drones was already pretty large. It was a win/win situation in an economic sense.

The Captain found it somewhat distasteful to use the drones in such a way. He found the policy of training them for war repugnant, but he followed his orders. The crawler reached the crash site and the passengers disembarked. The Doctor immediately hurried over to the wreck, noting where the blast marks were and assessing the damages. The woman was fairly dancing.

"See this, Captain? Right here. One shot punched through the intake of this craft and it couldn't compensate in time. It must have been flying rather low. From what is right in front of me, I would estimate that it was fired on while chasing a runner. Excellent, excellent," exhorted the Doctor. "We need to go to the other site immediately, Captain. Have your people load all of this on board for a more detailed analysis." She looked around briefly, "What is your MA officer's name again?"

"She is Officer Cutler, Doctor."

"Good, good. Any response from her in regard to the identity of the bodies? I am quite sure this is the work of my subject, but proof is required," the Doctor groused as she stepped back into the crawler.

The Captain waved his men back on board. It was a short jaunt to the clearing. The Doctor leapt out as the vehicle came to a stop. Efforts to keep a guard on the lady were frustrating to say the least. The woman had pulled up a map on her data pad that displayed all the locations of the bodies. The Captain decided to stay inside the crawler this time as the Doctor bounced around the kill site. She stopped and checked every spot where each body had been found.

The comm went off in the Captain's ear, "Captain? Come in, Captain."

"Officer Cutler? This is the Captain. What may I do for you?"

"Positive ID on one Jimmy Trudow. He is one of the missing prisoners from the Vogelgesang accident."

"I am quite certain that ship did not suffer an accident. Thank you for the information."

He flipped the comm off and turned to find the Doctor uncomfortably close to him, "You have a positive ID, yes?"

"Yes, Doctor. One of the escapees from the prison ship."

"The body that came in parts? Excellent, excellent," the woman muttered excitedly as she sat back inside the crawler. "Do we have a lead on where she went next, Captain?"

The Captain replied stoically, "My people are checking all the ship manifests from around the time of the police report. We have verified that there is a bit of a hole in the paper trail of one ship. No manifest on file for a cargo container being shipped off world, but the local union has a delivery certificate for it." He looked down at his data pad, "We should have more information soon."

"Good, good, Captain. My blood is up and we are close!" The Doctor whispered, mostly to herself, "So close I can taste it." She turned back to stare at the Captain in a distinctly unsettling way, "Make all due haste, Captain."

"Of course, Doctor. Of course."

twenty

One Whole Hour

Galena walked in to the secondary engine room near the hangar bay and came across Barney as he was wiring in the cloaking device. She set down a few bags, found a box to sit on and stretched out her legs. She moaned slightly as her legs unkinked and she settled in more comfortably.

Barney regarded her from the corner of his eye, "Busy day shopping, hey? Did Jacquie and Luli come back with you?"

"This shopping thing can really take a toll. My legs are killing me," she remarked. "No, the two die-hards are both still out there. They met up with some pilot friend of Luli's." She shifted to look into her bags. "The Captain says I should now be fully outfitted for regular space duty... and shore leave."

Jon Gray Lang

Barney tied up the last wire and sat back on his haunches, "Did those two wear you out?"

"Yes. They did. The whole undertaking was a first for me... spending my own mazuma, making choices as to what I need or want... or even what looks good on me! Such a strange idea, that last one. I've never been asked if I like something or been told that this or that color works on me. It's all very bewildering!" She threw her arms up in the air.

He laughed and leaned back, "You'll get used to it. You might not ever care about it, but you'll get used to it. Have any other plans for the day?"

She thought for a moment, "Not really. I still don't know what I should do when I'm on board. I have a very particular set of skills and most of them don't seem to transfer over to ship duty... or what I think of as ship duty."

"You'd be surprised lass, you'd be surprised." He stretched as he stood up, "I could use some help up here and I can think of a ton of tasks where having another set of hands and eyes about would speed things up. I got that hatch replaced finally, but there are always other things that need tweaking and the like."

Galena's eyes lit up at the thought. It was hard for someone who had been built for labor to know what to do with down time. She stood, put her fist over her chest and said solemnly "I am willing to assist in any way you see fit."

He laughed again, "My, you are a serious one. For now, I just need someone to flip that switch over there on and off when I ask. It saves me having to get up and down. My knees aren't what they used to be, you know." He turned to hunker down and connect his data pad to a port on the Plasma Cloak Generator, "Keep a watch on the power indicator, would you?"

She moved up next to the switch he had indicated and got comfortable. She asked a few questions about what she should keep an eye on and what else needed to be done. For now, it was just testing to see how much power drain the device would cause and if the ship was even capable of providing that power.

"Turn it on again."

She flicked the switch and stared at the indicator while she asked a little timidly, "Barney? Can I ask you a question?"

"Yeah, sure," he replied. "Okay, turn it off. What was the draw?"

"It was just over the parameters you gave me." She looked away from the indicator, "How did you end up on the Matilda?"

He stopped to give her a penetrating look. "I'll give you a choice. Do you want to know how I came to be on board or do want to know more about this boat?" He turned back to his data pad and adjusted some signal levels, "Turn it back on."

She flipped the switch, watched the power indicator and contemplated his question, "Before I decide, how much do you know about this ship and its origin?"

"Thought the choice might pique your interest. Turn it off." He fiddled with the power settings. "Of everyone on board, I have been on this ship the longest." He gave her a glance, "To give you part of an answer, my brother paid the first family that owned this ship a high price to smuggle me off my home world of Titan. That was a few hundred years ago, depending on which planet you're using to measure time. Turn it on."

"You make this choice very difficult, Mr. de Lagnel. I guess... tell me what you know about the ship?"

"Turn it off. Where's the fun in easy?" He gave her a grin and continued, "As I was saying, my brother paid to get me off planet so I could escape my near certain future. And it's a debt I'll never be able to repay. They smuggled me on board in a sleeper tube hidden under a delivery of grains of all things. It took me forever to get the stuff out of every nook and cranny." He looked up at her, "Turn it back on again. I was released from the sleeper tube after we went through the system gate. I was still young for my kind, only in my thirties and quite inquisitive. The Tiwi's were a very nice family and they gave me the run of the ship. They asked me where I wanted to be dropped off, but I knew next to nothing of the galaxy. Those of my ilk don't need to know much 'to serve their purpose' as our priests would say."

"The Tiwi's? Isn't that the bounty hunter's name?"

"Huh? Oh yes. It was his great grandfather who got me off Titan. Did you know that Derain was named after him? Anyway, I started following him around, the great grandfather, not the bounty hunter. He was the patriarch of the family at the time, but he was more inclined toward the mechanical side. He eventually took me on as an apprentice, as it were, and here I still am. Turn it off."

Barney punched at his data pad for a few moments. "He had been part of the salvage crew that had found the Matilda. From the story he told me, it had been open to space and completely abandoned. They found it on the edge of the Tiburon system. It's a pretty dead system, if you haven't been there. There have been exploration missions out there since, but nothing else has been found. No one knows where the ship came from or how it got there or even why it was open to space. Okay, turn it back on."

He continued, "For the salvage crew, it was pay day. They couldn't locate a living owner; the ship's records had been wiped and, from all appearances, she was in good working order. Tiwi decided to opt in for the ship and get out of the salvage business. It took his life savings plus the cut he had earned, but the Matilda was now his. Okay, turn it off. What are the readings?"

"Within the parameters, but still on the high end," she replied. She had become very focused on the story and imagined a younger version of Derain bringing his family on board this ship to explore space. "Will you tell me more?"

"I didn't say I was done yet, now did I?" he retorted. "Well anyway, he brought his extended family on board. His sister, Binda, was a trained pilot and they took off to become rich merchants. Being a merchant didn't turn out to be as easy as they expected, but they did well enough; well enough to feed another mouth. This is when I was smuggled aboard. Our neighborhood bounty hunter's great grandfather had been just a young fellow. Okay, turn it back on."

He checked his data pad, "Now turn it back off. Where was I? Oh yes. That jump engine stumped him and it became his focus. And because he was my teacher, it became my focus, too. He eventually died of old age and afterward, his son flew the ship for years. His wife... what was her name? Yaru, that's it. Yaru didn't like the merchant's life and wanted to raise their children on a planet. With a heavy heart, Mullion Tiwi, son of Derain Tiwi, sold the ship and moved to Aketi. Turn it on. How is the reading now?"

Galena looked down at the indicator, "It's pretty close to the optimal. So... the jump engine was already on board the ship?"

"Hmm? Yes. It was on board when

the ship was originally salvaged." He turned toward her with a face filled with glee, "I actually have Luli involved now, too. She's been trying to pull the ghosted records prior to the wipe to see where it came from." His data pad beeped, "Go ahead and turn it off."

He opened a panel in the device casing and pulled out a connector, "I stayed aboard under the next three owners. Let's see, there was Captain Kartis, until she sold the ship to Captain Arias. That man was always a bit of a fool. He flew it until he lost it in a game of chance to Captain Sawdey. He eventually sold it to the Delahaye's." He pulled his head out of the casing and turned to look at her, "Oh, they were such a young couple when Jacquotte was born, but she was such a surprise and a delight." A wistful smile crossed his face, "I can still remember how tiny she was and always giggling. As serious as she's become since taking command, it's good to see her be able to be happy again."

He stood up and wiped his hands on his pants, "That should just about do it. The only thing left is a real time test off planet."

Galena's expressions went from thoughtful, to calculated, to confused, to end up shocked.

He replaced the casing cover and looked over at her, "That went relatively smooth." He looked quizzically at her, "Why the look? What is it?"

"I have only one question. Why did

you need to escape your home world? Were you some sort of criminal?" she asked.

"What? No! I was going to be sold into the sex trade!" Barney chortled.

twenty-one

Turkey in the Straw

With the hatch replaced and the work on the cloaking device as done as it could be with the ship on the ground, Barney declared the repairs on the ship complete. Galena had headed back to her cabin and slid the parts that Anton had requested into the vent. She heard a muffled "Thanks!" before she headed off to the lounge. After she got comfortable, she scrolled through more of the Consortium's history on her brand new data pad. Jacquie wandered in through the hatch, followed shortly by Luli.

"Are we keeping this evening short... or who wants to go back out after dinner?" Jacquie keyed the ship's comm, "Barney? You want to head out tonight? You've been cooped up in here too long."

Galena looked up, "He should have some free time. We got quite a lot done today."

"Barney, I hear you got a lot done today. It's time to celebrate!" She looked over at Galena, "That means you, too."

"Umm, okay Captain." she replied as Luli laughed in the background.

"Luli, isn't it your turn to cook?" Jacquie asked. Luli thought a moment and nodded in the affirmative. "Good. Teach our new crew member the how to's on that." With a wry smile, "Time to earn your downtime keep. I'm off to the fresher. See you soon."

Luli looked over at Galena, "Okay you. Time to learn to cut onions! I've got to wash my hands."

***

Barney made his way up a while later to wonderful smells that wafted from the galley. He had put on one of his better outfits for the evening and was prepared for a bar crawl kind of a night. Any time they were stuck in port for more than a week, Jacq wanted to cut loose with the whole crew. From what he could tell, tonight was the night.

He came around the corner to find Luli and Galena deep in conversation while the Captain spoke with the commander of the mercenary police force over the comm. Derain still hadn't returned and Anton was still hidden inside the walls of the ship, a place he made sure everyone knew he hated. He set the table for the four of them and took his place. It wasn't long before Galena joined him as Luli brought over the meal.

"Dinner's ready, mon Capitan. Finish that call!" admonished Luli.

Jacquie made a face as she shut the comm off and took her place at the table. "Shush you. Such insubordination, but I'll forgive you for the smell of this meal alone. Is this the produce you picked up earlier? You're giving Rabbit a run for his money." She turned aside to Galena, "Anton prides himself on being the best cook on board." She looked away for a moment, "Or did anyway."

The table reverberated to the give and take of insults and jokes. It was the first time that Galena felt like a member of the crew instead of a hangers on. She reveled in the feeling and hoped it would would never end.

After everyone had finished eating, Jacquie addressed the group, "I worked a deal with the local mercs to speed up our release. I gave them the salvage rights to that ship and the case is now closed. Truth be told, they weren't really making any headway with it and we need to get a move on. Can't make the currency if we just sit in port." She turned to Barney, "From what Galena told me earlier, we should be good to go for departure. Anything holding us up?"

"The Lieutenant is correct. We can be ready to leave whenever we need to." He winked at her, "Just give the command and, as Luli would say, we're off into the wild blue yonder!"

***

Anton listened as the crew disembarked from the Matilda and knew he was alone once more. It was alright, though. He had his personal project to attend to. It was nice to be armed again... or soon to be armed, anyway. As he slid the safety switch back into position just above the grip, he heard a knock on the small hatch. This was the same hatch that gave access to the service hole he was hidden in. Only the crew knew about the existence of it so he walked over to open it without any concerns.

***

"This man is heavy!" yelled Galena.

After a long night of dancing, drinking and more dancing, the crew of the Matilda decided to make a morning of it as the second sun broke the horizon. Barney had gotten drunk... drunk to the point of passing out and Galena was trying to carry him back to the ship... through her own drunken haze. She wore the outfit that Luli had told her to wear and she had felt, what was the word Jacquie used? Pretty? Yes, that was it. She had felt pretty. Such a strange feeling. It made her uncomfortable, but she felt stronger at the same time. Of course she felt quite a bit different now with a dwarf sized person on her back who must weigh an absolute ton.

Luli laughed as she tripped in the mud and fell flat on her face. Jacquie giggled when she also lost her footing and fell on her ass. This caused Galena to laugh and she dropped Barney in another puddle.

All three of them were laughing as Barney woke up spluttering mud in all directions. "What in the nine hells is going on? Why did you throw me in the mud!" He grabbed her ankle and pulled, dropping her on her face in the mud. The gales of laughter that erupted at this point awakened somebody who yelled for them to shut up.

The lot of them walked aboard the Matilda dripping mud and erupting in fits of giggles. Following Jacquie, they filed into the med lab to switch into some clothing that wouldn't be a pain to clean up afterward. Jacquie knocked on the wall and asked Anton how his night was, but there was no response. She knocked again and still there was no answer. A somber mood struck the room as Jacquie ran to the small hatch.

She came back out and told everyone, "He's gone and the hatch is wide open. I think someone grabbed him."

"I'll check the camera records to see who boarded while we were gone," Luli said as she stepped out and ran to the lift.

Barney pulled his pants up, "I'll grab

my box. Lieutenant, you may want to prepare for a rescue mission."

Galena stood uncertainly for a moment before she followed Luli to the lift.

Now Jacquie stood alone in the empty bay and she whispered in frustration, "Damn it."

twenty-two

Sixteen Tons

After receiving the high priority 'no questions asked' code set, the crew of the Zangspur system jump gate waived the unmarked ship through. The Captain of the M33 was aware that news would eventually spread of their arrival, but it would take a while.

Lieutenant Hayley, lost in concentration suddenly blurted, "Captain, I am picking up a lot of chatter... chatter about a salvage."

"Track it. Navigation, get a fix on the salvage operation and set our heading," he ordered.

The communications officer continued," Ship is unmarked... unknown configuration... multiple bodies found so far... damage to communications on exterior... at least one damaged engine." He turned to the Captain, "These reports are from the local police force."

"I have a lock, sir. Heading changed to 351-mark-10," stated Navigation.

"One outer hatch destroyed... blast marks down multiple corridors... reports of multiple interior hatches pulled from their hinges... includes bridge hatch..." She turned to the Captain, "Sir, the reports seem to indicate a massive firefight onboard the ship." She listened for a moment then continued, "The ship appears to have been opened to space before the firefight started... weapons lockers were emptied and something large was removed from the ship's engine room... unknown configuration."

This derelict was either the ship they were seeking or another victim, another breadcrumb as the Doctor would say, on the trail to her prize. The Captain brooded as he wondered what kind of beast they were chasing. His ship came within hailing range of the wreck as the salvage crews' lights played on the surface of the hull.

"Sir? We are receiving requests for identification."

"Maintain audio silence," he commanded.

The scanner technician added, "From the ship's configuration, it appears to be one of ours."

The Captain brooded audibly before he gave the order he had hoped he wouldn't have to give, "Communications, cut off their feed. Gunnery, target the salvage ships and open fire."

"Sir! Yes, sir!" rang through the bridge. He felt the deck vibrate as the guns fired. "Inform me when the intruders are expunged. You have the bridge, Lieutenant." He stood and left his underlings to manage the cleanup.

Sometimes he regretted his choice to join the Black Ops branch. The rules were quite clear on the retrieval of their tech. No one but the branch could know anything about the technology in their ships, especially the FTL drives. No exceptions could be given. If the Doctor's pet had been onboard that ship, then its life was forfeit as well.

If the Doctor's pet had been responsible for what the reports indicated, what kind of monster would his people face? What type of drone can tear hatches open? What had the Doctor built? He felt it was time to demand some answers.

twenty-three

Sinner Man

Jacquie stood behind Luli as she cycled through the Matilda's camera feeds. They searched the footage for any sign of Anton's departure... and who may have forced him to leave the ship.

"Hold! I think I saw something from Camera Three. Scroll back," ordered the Captain.

"Aah. I see what you're talking about," Luli interjected. "Whoever this is, they know where the cameras are."

Galena and Barney edged forward as Luli accelerated through the feeds to see Anton being led away. "Looks like his wrists are tied and he is definitely blindfolded."

"Who's with him?" asked Barney.

"Still looking for a good angle on the

face... wait a minute. I got him!" crowed Luli. "What? It can't be? This can't be right."

Jacquie's face dropped into a scowl as her hands clenched.

"Who is it?" asked Galena.

"It's Derain," deadpanned the Captain. "Luli, pull his comm records and look for anything... anything at all. Damn it, I need a drink."

Barney followed Jacquie to the lounge as Galena slid up behind Luli. The Lieutenant asked, "Is it really the bounty hunter?"

Luli conceded, "It sure is. No one else walks like that."

"Are you surprised to find it was him? Does he not sell people?" she asked tentatively.

Luli turned to look at her incredulously, "He doesn't sell people; he turns them in for bounties... Oh my! You're brilliant, Ms. Chadov!"

Galena looked on in bewilderment as Luli keyed the comm, "Captain, we've got a break through! What big crime boss was trying to nab Rabbit earlier?"

"Ah ha! Good work, Ms. Qing. See if you can pinpoint a location for Mr. Leon's operation on this dirtball of a planet. Everyone else, suit up! We're going hunting!"

It hadn't taken Luli very long to call in a couple of debts to find out where this Mr. Leon held court. The Folly backed out of the Matilda's cargo bay and the crew was on their way.

"Do we know what sort of a layout the place has?" Barney queried.

"I've only been able to pull some sketchy information on the site," responded Luli. "Five story structure and it's relatively old, almost colonial." She looked back at him, "You would think there would be more information on the net about it. Looks as if a lot of the records were purged."

"So we're going in with no idea how much firepower we'll be facing, where Anton is, or even if he's in the building," he stated.

"You don't have to go in, Barney." retorted Jacquie.

"What? You know me, I love a challenge!" he grumbled in response.

Galena could feel the tension in the air of the vehicle... tension along with an almost fierce joy she hadn't felt since... well, since the ship that attacked them, really. She stared out the window as they cruised by the building they would be entering soon... in the most nonchalant of manners. Captain Delahaye parked the Folly close to the building.

She watched as Barney hit a switch which slid the floor panel away. Right below the crawler was a sewer lid. He hooked a rod into the lid and slid it out of the way. A glow stick dropped from his hand into the opening before he turned to her and yelled, "Where he goes, no one knows!" His laughter echoed down the shaft until he landed. She steeled herself and leapt in after him.

Jon Gray Lang

"Gods, I hate these kinds of entrances." uttered the Captain as Luli landed next to her.

"They do have a certain je ne sais quoi, don't they?" Barney growled in response. "Let's get on with this. Which way, Lu?"

Luli straightened as she checked her HUD and pointed directly ahead. "Straight on. There should be an old shaft off to the left." She looked around the sewer tunnel, "This structure is a lot older than I thought. There might actually be a door there."

"I'll take point," Galena said as she ghosted into the darkness ahead of them.

Barney looked over at the two women, "She knows her stuff, eh? This should be fun!" He took off after her.

"Should we be concerned that he's getting excited?" quipped Luli.

They followed quickly behind. There was a doorway to the sewer just where Luli said one might be. The entrance could just be made out behind a wall of crumbling old bricks. They looked at each other and nodded before they set to and tore that wall down. Once it was cleared and the door opened, the light from their headlamps was barely enough to reveal the bottom of a staircase ahead.

By the time they got to the top of the short staircase, Barney had rigged a viewing contraption to the door.

"Looks clear," he said as he put the

device away. Galena fiddled with the lock when an audible click echoed in the staircase. Luli smirked and raised a single finger to her lips. As Barney cracked the door, Galena peeked out and did a quick scan of the hall that lay on the other side of their position. She signaled the all clear and everyone entered the hall.

"Next level should be accessible right around... there," Luli pointed.

They all crept toward an old service elevator that remained unguarded. Once everyone had stepped inside, Luli hit the top floor button. As the team rode the lift up, she jacked into the small brain of the elevator and bypassed the password requirements. Galena slid to the other side of the elevator door opposite from Luli and took a few deep calming breaths.

"If I had an office in this grand old building, I'd want the best view, right?" pondered Luli. "From the records, it looks like that would be the third door to the left."

"It's a destination, so it's good enough for me. Everyone on your toes," commanded the Captain.

The elevator doors slid open to another empty hallway that angled to the left. Galena stepped lightly to the corner and spied a single guard. She waved the others back, bolted down the hall and struck the guard in the head with her elbow. She caught him as he collapsed. She waved the others forward as she slid him out of the way.

Barney muttered under his breath as he opened the doors to their supposed office destination, "I'm glad we ran into some opposition. I was beginning to think that it was some kind of trap..."

There were armed men to the left and to the right of their little group as the door swung slowly open. Jacquie stewed over their situation as they were led into the office. The doors closed behind them while they took in the room.

There was easily triple the manpower facing them than what they had brought in. They were simply outgunned. A small, unremarkable looking man sat behind a desk while Derain was perched in a chair facing him. There was no doubt that it was the bounty hunter from the queue that pulled his hair back. Anton smirked at them all as he lounged on the corner of the desk.

"You were quite correct, Mr. Tiwi. Very punctual," exclaimed the man behind the desk. "Please, please, make yourselves comfortable. We are in the midst of a negotiation." He paused for a moment, "Oh yes, and thank you for demonstrating one of the weaknesses of my home. I had forgotten about that old entrance. Refreshment?"

The guards lowered their weapons once Jacquie gave the order for her people to relax. Mr. Leon's men exited the room until only the crew of the Matilda was left with the infamous gangster.

Galena stepped forward and gave the

man a long appraising gaze. "You are familiar to me. I feel that I have seen you before or that I should know you."

Barney immediately interrupted with a drink in one hand, "What a view! You guessed right, Luli! This is the place for an office." He turned to Mr. Leon, "I like your sense of style. Oh and this is very good. I haven't had any since I left Titan," indicating the drink.   "You want some, Anton?"

Anton waved him off as Luli approached him, "Everything alright, Rabbit?"

Jacquie stood in the middle of the room and everyone could feel the tension that radiated from her. "Could someone please explain to me what sort of a negotiation we are involved in?" She turned toward the desk, "Should I be concerned for my people, Mr. Leon?"

"Please sit down, sit down."   He waved her over, "Let me tell you a story that your Mr. Tiwi relayed to me."   Mr. Leon paused a moment as he gathered his thoughts. "I received a petition which said that the gentleman here was trying to locate a bounty for your friend over there. This was much to my surprise as I had no clue who your Mr. Rabbit was."

"Just Rabbit, thanks," Anton piped in.

"Of course.   My apologies," he replied. "Needless to say, my curiosity was piqued. Why would this Mr. Tiwi assume that I had a warrant out for this person? It took some digging, but my people found a wiped delivery record and rumors of a recently gutted ship in our lovely system. Favors were called in and I eventually requested a meeting with your compatriots, Mr. Tiwi and Mr. Roane."

"You aren't the one who put out the contract on Anton?" asked Jacquie. "Then why did you lead him out of my ship as a prisoner, Derain?"

As Derain was about to answer, Mr. Leon spoke again, "Allow me to answer for your crewman, Ms. Delahaye. In my investigation, I had come across information that your ship had been bugged. During my conversation with Mr. Tiwi, we came to the conclusion that your ship must have been bugged at the time it was boarded. Now I come to the point in the story where I explain to you why I care about your ragtag bunch, Captain. I want to know who is using my name without my approval. So this, all of this, is an elaborate ruse..."

"To tip off those who are looking for Anton that he would be here." Jacquie looked at her people, one by one. "We are the bait for his trap." She turned back to look into the pale green eyes of the small man, "So what is the plan now, Mr. Leon? Do we get to leave intact?"

"Oh, but of course, Captain. I have need of your services," he chortled. "I already had the bugs stripped from your ship and I have provided Mr. Tiwi the destination for the delivery of my goods."

"You brokered a deal under my

nose?"

Derain calmly replied, "It was a rushed job. I'm sorry about this Jacq. I found out about most of this just before you got here."

"Mr. Leon, why should we deliver your goods? Why don't my people and I just leave now?" she asked.

At that moment, a man cracked the door to the room, "Excuse me sir, your expected guests have arrived. I would recommend closing out this meeting as soon as possible."

"Quite right. To answer your question, Captain, they've already been placed on board your ship and I would recommend you leaving Zangspur as soon as possible."

Gunfire could be heard coming from below. Screams and minor explosions rumbled under the floor as well.

"Bigger guns," muttered Barney.

"Captain, I do think we should head out now," Derain stated as he stood.

"My ship. If they tracked us then they'll be on my ship."

"Not to worry, Captain. I took the liberty to have your ship's berth changed once my cargo was loaded on board." He stood up and shooed them toward a side door as the gunfire grew closer and louder. "Time is of the essence. You'll find the elevator you arrived in a level down. Please, do be careful." He paused as the last of them piled through the door, "Till we meet again."

Jon Gray Lang

Jacquie turned to face him, "Do you have a way out?"

The other set of doors exploded inward and Mr. Leon spun to face them. Gunfire raked the room and nearly cut him in half. Jacquie stared in horror through the crack of the door.

"Do not fear for me, for we are legion..." gasped Mr. Leon as he slid to the floor.

twenty-four

Blister in the Sun

The crew scurried back through the tunnel to the Folly parked above their heads. They clambered back inside and shut the floor entrance when an explosion tore a chunk out of the building they had vacated just minutes ago.

"Nice," exclaimed Anton.

"You. Stay out of sight," commanded the Captain. "Luli, get us out of here."

Anton raised his hands in mock surrender, and then hunkered down into a corner.

"Where am I going, Derain?" asked Luli as Jacquie locked herself in.

"Berth 72."

"On it. Everyone try to look casual. Looks like they've got this place locked down," Luli said quietly. Another explosion rocked the building.

Luli pushed the Folly into traffic on the main street. The feeling of faked nonchalance was palpable as the runner rolled past the old building that had been, until now, Mr. Leon's home operation. The place crawled with soldiers; not the local merc police force, but true to form Consortium troopers. The building had been cordoned off and prisoners already were being led into a back alley. Galena watched as prisoners were lined up, shots were fired and bodies were loaded into bags. More body bags were stacked off to the side as the runner rolled out of viewing range.

Jacquie whispered tersely, "Anton, you must explain to us why what appears to be a Consortium Special Forces team is after you."

Luli brought the crawler around to Berth 72 and to her unmistakable relief, the Matilda was there. Everyone exited the Folly and it was quickly strapped down in place. Jacquie spied a new stack of containers secured to the decking. There was a small package with a note placed on top. She opened the small box to find a pile of listening devices and cameras. She quickly handed them off to Barney as he passed by on his way to the engine room.

"Luli, get us set for lift off. The faster we're away from here, the sooner we can lose Rabbit's friends," she muttered as she opened the handwritten note. "Lieutenant, please join Luli up top as you'll be on weapons. Derain, wait a moment."

Derain exhaled as he walked over to the Captain and steeled himself for a berating. Her eyes pierced into him in a way no other woman's ever had. The sensation was unnerving. She smiled and that little quirk appeared in the corner of her mouth.

"Thanks again, Derain. Your quick thinking saved us from losing just about everything that matters to me." She raised the bit of paper, "This handwritten note says you got us a high paying gig, too." He stiffened then relaxed as she gave him a hug. "Why you stick with us is beyond me sometimes, but I love you for it." She released him, "I might need the Waratah to run interference. You think you can prep her on the move?"

Anton interrupted, "I'll help him out, Jacq. Come on Mr. Bounty Hunter, sir. Do you not feel the beckoning of adventure?"

The ship rumbled under the Captain's feet as Luli's voice cracked over the comm, "Captain, we've been given the go to leave. Everyone buckle in!" Jacquie ran to the lift and keyed it for the top deck.

***

As Derain belted into the Waratah, he turned to Anton, "You are Gunnery rated, correct?" Anton nodded an affirmative and Derain continued, "Just so you know, I'm almost dead certain I saw your prisoner friend back there. It seemed like he was in charge of a bunch of those troops."

"You mean Sam? You must be mistaken. He was more Johnny Reb than I ever was," Anton distractedly replied as he keyed up the weapons system of the Waratah. "Wow. This is one hell of a ship you've got here."

"I could be wrong. I only saw him for a brief moment. Figured you might want to know," Derain concluded as he pulled up the release procedures.

"I don't think half of this stuff is legal in any system! Huh? Oh right, thanks. I don't see how it could've been him, though. Those were some heavy hitters," Anton replied.

"This is gonna be a bumpy ride. Make sure you're strapped in tightly, Rabbit."

"This aint my first rodeo, Derain."

***

Jacquie keyed the ship to ship comm, "Derain, once we break atmo, I'll open the hangar bay doors." She turned to Galena, "Any chatter about us leaving?"

"Nothing so far, sir. We're breaking atmo now."

"No need for sirs on this boat, Lieutenant," she grinned. She switched to the in ship comm, "Barney, I've got a bad feeling something planet side is tracking us. How do you feel about a field test on the cloak? Being able to vanish may come in real handy."

He speculated before he keyed the comm back, "No time like the present, I suppose. I'll queue it up." He muttered to himself, "What's the worst that could happen... besides it exploding?"

"I heard that Mr. de Lagnel," the Captain replied. "Cut all the chatter, folks. As Luli would say, let's pretend we're the Green Fairy off to deliver toys to the galaxy's good girls and boys."

***

Scanner Technician Cordelan turned to the Captain, "Sir, a cargo ship just left the planet's gravity well."

"Configuration?" asked Captain Kaplean.

"Unknown make, sir."

Doctor Wyeth interrupted, "Don't let that ship leave, Captain. You military types have made a hash of this situation. She has to be on board that trawler."

"Mind yourself, Doctor. Lieutenant Hayley, any chatter from the surface?"

"All signals appear to be jammed, sir."

Doctor Wyeth started up again, "Isn't that the modus operandi of your branch, Captain? Squeeze so tight that everything slips through the cracks? My genorg is slipping away as we stand here and do nothing!"

"Doctor, please leave my bridge. We

will contact you once we have the vessel," the Captain shot back curtly. "Helm, change course heading to match. Gunnery, prepare to disable that ship."

The Captain ignored Doctor Wyeth as the woman left in a fit of pique.

***

"Uh, Jacquie? We just got pinged by a ship out there that's trying to match our trajectory," Luli stated.

"Dammit. Keep an eye on it, Lu. Lieutenant, get a target lock on that boat."

***

Scanner Technician Cordelan reported, "They've made no change to their course, sir."

Captain Kaplean ordered, "Helm, keep to our course heading."

***

"Is it just me or does that ship look a lot like the one we dealt with when we entered this system?" Luli queried.

Galena checked her board, "Looks the same to me."

"Me too," Jacquie said. She keyed the

comm to the Waratah, "Prepare for a fight Derain. Looks like it's the same team. Anton? Why does the whole bloody Consortium want you so badly? What did you do?"

**

Anton shrugged helplessly after the comm dropped.   Derain gave him a derisive look and went back to work powering up the ship's engines.

**

"Galena, when they come in range, take out their communications array," ordered Jacquie. "The last thing we need is even more of these bastards after us. Lu, you know the drill. Evasives on firing."

"But of course! I am a fighter jock, mon Capitan. I feel the wind beneath my wings!"

**

Scanner Technician Cordelan spoke up, "Captain, I am registering a new heat source coming from the target. Possible small engine based craft."

"Have we pegged the configuration on that vessel?" he asked.

The scanner technician replied, "No

sir. The design is not recognized by our database."

***

"That ship will be in range in moments, Captain. I have a target lock on their comm tower. Missiles loaded for hull spread," declared Galena.

"Waratah, launch!" commanded Jacquie. "Fire the spread, Lieutenant."

The Matilda shuddered as the missiles left their tubes. Galena fired three rounds from the coil guns toward the mystery ship.

***

The Waratah shot out of the hangar as the catapult system hurled it toward the other ship.

"Wahoo!" bellowed Anton.

"Will you shush for a moment? We're just here as a distraction! See what you can throw at them that will deceive their sensors!" Derain snapped. "For now!"

***

"A small ship, troop lander configuration, inbound sir," divulged Scanner Tech Cordelan. "I think it's firing on us?"

***

Anton crowed as he hit the firing switch and the Waratah shot over the bow. As the round rocketed over the hull of the government ship he yelled, "That should keep 'em busy!"

***

"Keep on the target, Cordelan," replied the Captain.

"Five small objects inbound, Captain! Their heat signature was mixed with the one from the small ship!" cried the scanner technician.

"Target locked and missile away, sir." came the guttural voice of Gunnery Alavarez.

"Good work, Gunnery," affirmed the Captain as the incoming missiles impacted on the hull of his ship. Once again he wondered what kind of fiend they were chasing. Its team had some serious audacity. That was most certain.

"We've lost our communications array, Captain," replied Lieutenant Hayley.

"Are we still on target, Gunnery?" asked the Captain.

"Yes, sir."

The ship rocked from an explosion and alarms blared in response.

Gunnery Alvarez stated, "That was an explosion in Weapons Tube 7, sir. The fire crew is en route. That was an..."

Jon Gray Lang

***

"... amazing shot, Galena!" Jacquie cheered as the eruption lit up the board then quickly dissipated.

"Dropping chaff now," Luli stated.

***

Derain brought the Waratah hard about, but it didn't slow her much. "Anton! Once we pass the sublight engines, throw as many concussives into it as you can!"

***

"Firing secondary on matched trajectory," affirmed Gunnery Alvarez.

Captain Kaplean keyed the comm, but there was no response. He turned to Yeoman Fitzpatrick, "Please inform Chief Bull to launch when ready." The Yeoman saluted and ran for the lift.

"Sir, I am getting damage reports from the hangar bay. One of the impacts mangled the bay doors."

"Thank you, Mr. Cordelan."

***

Jon Gray Lang

The Waratah flew past the aft of the attacking ship and launched a barrage of concussive missiles into two of the sublight engine cones. There was a bright flare and one of the engines went dark. The other flickered, but didn't go out completely.

***

Luli pulled hard, but she couldn't shake the missile. It had bypassed the chaff and was intent on slamming into her ship. "Damn smart missiles! May Tom take you to the abyss!"

***

There was a plume of light; then it went dark. The Gunnery grunted in satisfaction and tracked his second missile. "She's hurt, Captain. Secondary disabling missile should arrive within the minute."

"Thank you, Gunnery." Captain Kaplean turned to his pilot, "Are we still on course?"

"We've lost two engines, so she's sluggish, but we're still on course."

***

"How bad is it?" asked Captain Delahaye as she was thrown back into her seat.

"I've still got her under control, but

she turns like a brick!" an exasperated Luli shouted.

"Lieutenant, you have free will to fire. Let's get this thing off our backs."

***

Derain slowed the Waratah's momentum as he brought her about. "How many do we have left?"

Anton checked the ship inventory, "We've got five left. Go for broke?"

"Do it." Derain keyed the ship to ship comm, "Jacq, not much more we can do out here; on our way back."

***

"Swinging out to meet up with you. Going to be a rough one. Be careful out there," declared Luli.

"Two more shots away, Captain," Galena announced.

***

The Waratah adjusted its angle as it continued to rocket away from the attacking ship. The Matilda cut a wide arc to bring it closer to the Waratah. The two ships were almost flying circles around each other. Anton fired the remaining inventory at the unmarked craft just as their angle of attack became no longer viable. They watched the handful of small missiles impact on the ship's hull minutes later.

"Well, now we just wait," muttered Derain.

***

"Incoming!" screamed Luli as the Matilda was hit again. "Whoever their gunner is, they're a good shot!" The handling on the Matilda grew even more sluggish until only the small directional engines responded, "Lost the big ones, Jacq. Only have the maneuvering jets left."

"I thought so. How long till we rendezvous with the others?"

"Another ten minutes. We're dead in the water though.

Galena piped up, "I'll keep them wary of us."

***

His ship shuddered from the impacts of the small missiles. He checked his charts as he waited for confirmation from his gunner.

"Direct hit, sir."

The crunch of another impact rang on the bridge, "Thank you, Alvarez."

"They just hit our bow port!" exclaimed Lieutenant Hayley.

"Helm, turn us away, immediately!" yelled Captain Kaplean. Another impact shook the bridge as a small crack appeared in the plas-glass of the bow port.

In shock, Scanner Technician Cordelan yelled, "By the Major!"

***

"Lu? How much longer until the Waratah is back on board?" asked Jacquie.

"Countdown is five minutes. We're coasting now. Anything left on your end Galena?"

"The range is too far out now," she responded. "Not much else to do, but wait." She looked around, "Anyone have a deck of cards?"

***

Scanner Technician Cordelan piped up, "Defense systems aren't registering any other projectiles from the target." He pulled up trajectory reports from the battle, "That ship is too far out now. It shouldn't be able to load a successful strike against us."

"Shouldn't?" intoned the Captain.

Cordelan replied, "The vessel is an unknown, so this is an estimation at best, sir."

"Understood. Helm, regain a trajectory on that boat and keep us off their gunner," Captain Kaplean ordered. A "sir, yes sir,"

Jon Gray Lang

echoed from the helmsman before he turned to his Gunnery, "Alvarez, I need that ship stopped, but not dead. Is that possible at this range?"

"I wouldn't trust to it, sir. Get me closer and I can get it done."

Navigation stated, "Sir. I have tracked both craft and they are set to rendezvous."

"Helm, change course to meet. Gunnery, prepare to fire once that ship is in range."

***

The larger ship lumbered over to its new trajectory. The damage done by the Waratah had made it definitely less responsive. It would still be able to come into attack range when the two ships met, but the window was much shorter. Still, Jacquie worried that escape might not be possible this time. Then she remembered the Plasma Cloak Generator they had taken from the other ship.

She keyed the comm excitedly, "Barney! I completely forgot about that cloaking device! You get that thing up in working order yet?"

Barney's voice rang through the comm, "I said it was ready before we launched! Just tell me when you want it switched on!"

Galena looked over at Luli, "He sounds angry."

"He gets pretty agitated during these kinds of engagements," she quipped back.

Jacquie gave Luli a nonplussed stare

and asked, "Can you let Derain know that we might 'disappear' please?"

"But of course, mon Capitan!" Luli keyed the ship to ship comm, "Waratah. Be prepared for a magic trick! Repeat, be prepared for a magic trick!" She turned toward the Captain and swore, "By the ghost of Major Tom!"

***

Anton looked at Derain with a quizzical expression, "A magic trick? What the hell are they doing over there?"

***

Jacquie and Galena both turned as Mr. Leon stepped through the hatch.

"Do you have a plan to extricate my goods from this marauder?" he asked.

"You are dead!" stuttered Jacquie. "I watched you die!" She stood up and backed away from him, "How are you here and alive!" She turned to Luli, "Are we being gassed again?"

Galena gave him an appraising look, "I thought you looked familiar." She paused a moment as he smiled a secretive smile. "The rumors at the crèche said your model had been discontinued. Due to mental issues, if I recall."

"It was found that we didn't follow orders well after receiving a certain amount of training. It is good to see another of our kind off on its own, though." He gave her a small bow. He turned to Jacquie, "I was delivered as part of the cargo you have on board. Now back to the matter at hand. What is your proposal to escape from that... ah... another Consortium ship? You do seem to be quite popular with those who control the gates, Captain."

***

"We are in range. Firing now," said Gunnery Alvarez.

Captain Kaplean nodded. "Helm, stay on course. Yeoman, is there any news concerning the hangar bay repairs?"

Fitzpatrick, who had just returned to the bridge, responded breathlessly, "Repairs should be completed in a half hour, sir."

The Captain sank back into his chair, "That gives them time to dig in. Yeoman, please inform Chief Bull to take the genorg alive. The rest are expendable." Yeoman Fitzpatrick saluted and then took off for the lift.

***

Derain turned to Anton, "Ready for a rough landing?"

"I'm ready for a magic trick," he deadpanned.

Jon Gray Lang

twenty-five

Tomorrow Never Knows

Jacquie toggled the comm and yelled, "Now!"

Barney slapped the big button he had finished wiring that morning. The crew on board waited, but nothing seemed to happen.

"Is it working?" wondered Luli.

***

Anton looked at Derain and then back out the bow port, "Whoa. Where'd it go?"

***

Lieutenant Hayley spoke, "Sir, we have repaired the in ship comms."

Navigation Officer Grissom double

checked her instruments then looked out the bow port, "The target ship is gone."

***

The Waratah came in hot and slammed into the docking web. As the Matilda shuddered with her landing, Jacquie yelled, "Hit all the maneuver jets and take us out of their approach!" The ship strained as it changed its angle and dropped to starboard.

***

Gunnery Alvarez cursed under his breath as his shot traveled through where his target should have been... before it had disappeared, "It's a miss, sir."

"Mr. Cordelan, any sign of it?" the Captain leaned forward. The scanner technician gave a negative. "Eyes peeled everyone. Extrapolate all possible trajectories. We may have to take to shooting blind."

***

Derain announced over the ship to ship comm, "Hangar bay doors closed. We're on our way back."

Barney's voice overrode Derain's, "Watch the power drain! I have no idea how long this... dammit we're losing it!"

Mr. Leon spoke up from behind, "I do hope you have a Plan C... Captain."

Jacquie cursed and glared at the man, "We're down to last resorts here, mister."

***

"Sir! I have a sighting of the ship again! Their cloak is dropping!" the Scanner Technician exclaimed.

"Alvarez?"

Alvarez replied, "Already launched sir. Impact will be in T minus three minutes."

***

Jacquie turned to Luli, "How far is the drop off?"

Luli piped up as she pointed at Mr. Leon, "I keyed in the coordinates the dead version of that guy gave us. It's a couple systems away."

Jacquie keyed the comm, "Can we make a long one?"

Barney replied, "It'll be a strain; that thing uses something else for power."

"Let's get this over with, then," muttered Jacquie.

Just then Anton and Derain popped through the hatch and they both saw Mr. Leon at the same time. Anton already had his pistol drawn while

Derain backed up and pulled his. "How are you here?" they said in unison. "Aren't you dead?"

"Aha.   I finally understand your nickname, Mr. Roane. You do have quite the quick draw. It is nice to see you again, Mr. Tiwi, even if I am to die again," said Mr. Leon.

"Get us out of here!" commanded Jacquie.

***

Gunnery Alvarez tracked his latest missile as it cruised toward the target that had been more difficult to take down than he expected. There was no way it would escape again.

Scanner Technician Cordelan spoke up, "Sir?   I am getting some strange power fluctuations coming from that ship."

Captain Kaplean stared in shock as a sickly light appeared to bleed from the little craft. The existing space around it seemed to twist in on itself, then engulf the small freighter and pull it into itself.

Doctor Wyeth, who had come back onto the bridge at some point, muttered "Oh my."

Alvarez cursed loudly as his latest missile sailed blindly through the now empty space.

The entire bridge crew stared out the cracked bow port... at nothing.

twenty-six

Black Hole Sun

Mr. Leon immediately threw up. The weird sickly light leaked through the bow port and washed over the face of everyone on the bridge. Everything felt wrong, the air, the feel of the walls, even the ship's internal gravity. Luli turned from her equipment and glanced over at the man retching before her gaze fell on Derain.

A very green Derain said, "It doesn't get any easier, does it?"

"No, no it doesn't," moaned Jacquie.

Luli swayed a bit as she pulled up from her seat. While she tried to solidify her stance, she grumbled, "God, that smell! It is peculiar to me how even time seems altered here. Anyway, I've set our drop point as close to the rendezvous coordinates as possible. I just hope we won't reappear inside of another ship. Barney sent an update on what he could repair and we're down on mobility. Batteries are almost completely drained. We have just enough to keep life support up and running."

Mr. Leon spoke up from his hunched over position, "What just happened? What is this? Where are we?" He paused a moment to gather his thoughts, "What is the cause of that stench?"

Luli interrupted him. "As I was saying, we are going to need serious dry dock time." She walked toward the hatch and gesticulated wildly, "We've got about five days in this, where ever the hell we are, before we reenter known space. I'm going to check all the airlocks to make sure they are completely locked down. This is going to be an adventure..."

Anton looked shocked, "Five days? Those things will be on us inside of an hour!" He noted the troubled face of the Captain and added, "Uh, I'm right behind you Luli."

Jacquie rubbed her face as Galena excused herself to see what help she could give Barney. Derain found a section of wall to lean up against. Mr. Leon straightened slowly and he wiped at his mouth.

He fixed a searching gaze on Jacquie, "What did he mean by things?"

Derain chuckled with little mirth, "Oh, you'll find out soon enough," he murmured heavily. "Soon enough."

Jacquie turned to Mr. Leon, "I'll try to explain. We are no longer in our space; we are somewhere else... we don't really know where. This will be the longest trip through this 'other space' we've ever done. I'm not completely sure we'll survive it." She turned away and pointed at the bow port, "As for the 'things' that Rabbit mentioned, you'll be able to see them soon enough. Just what they are, we don't know. Your guess is as good as mine. They will try to get inside this ship, though."

She turned back to Mr. Leon and gave him a piercing glare, "And if they do, all of us are dead. All of us." She turned away from him and keyed her console, "Now if you'll excuse me, I need to see what we can do to survive this jaunt through madness. Derain? Will you give Mr. Leon a tour of our home? He's going to need it."

As the two of them left, they heard her fist slam against her workstation. Derain muttered, "This is gonna be a long voyage." He looked down at Mr. Leon, "Do you have a first name?"

"My makers never deigned to give me one," he replied. "Besides, I do enjoy the formal edge in my conversations. It gives everything a certain je ne sais quoi. Wouldn't you agree?"

"It does keep a certain level of separation in place, yes." He waved Mr. Leon into the lounge, "This is where we eat and hang out. We'll set up a bunk for you in here. I'm pretty sure no one will want to be alone on this trip. You've already found the lift. Deck Two has the gym and Deck One houses sickbay which is fully stocked for now."

The lounge filled with a sudden scratching sound that emanated from the outer hull. Mr. Leon looked out the viewport and saw something he wished he hadn't. It was wormlike, but had appendages. Its gaping mouth sucked and chewed at the viewport and he could see straight down its gullet. A heavy thud rang through the ship as grinding noises commenced.

Derain peered out the viewport then looked away. He turned to Mr. Leon and said, "I have to take care of something on my ship right now. Do you think you've got a handle on Matilda's layout?" He waited for the nod before he continued, "Any questions, uh, just hail anyone through the comm system, alright?" He backed away from Mr. Leon and headed off to the hangar bay.

Mr. Leon stood in the lounge and watched as the monster tried to eat its way through the ship's hull to get at him. With a shudder he turned away to sit at one of the tables. After he recovered from the initial shock of the beast, he said out loud, "Interesting. The jump capability of this ship is of a variant unknown to me. Very interesting indeed."

***

Galena happened upon Barney as he

hurried to the secondary engine room off the hangar bay. She stopped in front of him and offered her services. He just grunted and waved her on to follow him. As the lift came to the third deck, he stomped off to his cabin. He popped back out and gave her a once over, "Change into something you don't mind getting filthy." He popped back in and rummaged around his cabin.

"Everything I own is new, so I guess any of it would do," she opined to the open hatch.

He popped back out and threw a very ratty t-shirt at her. "Still have those pants from when we brought you in? Those should do just fine." He stumped back into his cabin as she ruminated a moment then walked off down the hall.

She came back to find him wearing an outfit that seemed to contain hundreds of pockets. He gave her another look and appraised her attire, noting that the pants were still stiff with her blood, "Good enough. Let's go." He grabbed his tool bag and headed back to the lift.

"I can carry that for you."

He smirked, "I doubt it, but here you go."

He waited as she struggled to lift the bag before he shooed her away and picked it up. "I'm stronger than you. Just accept that and move."

The grating racket grew ever louder as they walked through the hangar bay. She spied Derain over at his ship as he checked the tie downs before he pulled a long crate out of a side compartment.   Barney walked off into the secondary engine room and Galena quickened her pace to keep up. She stood at the hatch a moment before she strode into the room. It was strange to her how much she felt at home on this ship.

Barney's voice rang out in the small room as he threw her a headset. "You here to daydream or to help? Either's fine, I just need to know."

She grimaced as she caught them and put them on, "What do you need me to do?"

"See that big access plate there? Take it off the wall. It's going to get really loud in here."

***

Anton and Luli checked the side hatch located in the cargo bay. He turned to her, "Well that's the last one. All of them are in full lock down. Any thoughts on where we make our last stand, if it's needed?"

She frowned at him as she walked back to the lift. He had to hustle to catch up. She punched the lift button and waited until the door opened. He followed her in and gave her a side glance.

"You pissed at me, Lu?"

She turned to face him squarely before she ranted, "Mad at you? Why would I be mad at you? Could it be that I've been shot at more times than I can count since you've been back?

Could it be that it looks like just about everyone in this damned galaxy is after you... for some reason that you can't or won't explain?" She turned away and stared fixedly at the lift door.

"Lu, I haven't got a clue as to why the Consortium is after me. I mean, sure, I was part of a revolution against them, but they caught me. They stuck me in prison for three years! Everything I know is old news now." His hands dropped to his sides and his head hung low, "I can't even fathom why Sam was after me. We butted heads back on Tigron, but that's the last time I dealt with him."

Luli spoke in clipped terms, "Well you better figure it out or I'm going to leave you somewhere and no one else is going to know about it." She turned to face him, "It'll be like you just disappeared all over again."

The lift door opened and Luli stepped out and left him standing alone. The decision he had made years ago had not only put himself in danger, but everyone he cared about as well... and they suffered for it. They were suffering for it right now. "What could I possibly know that anyone would care about? What do they want from me?"

Derain came around the corner to find Anton standing in an empty lift, talking to himself. He gave Anton a weird look as he continued on his way. Anton followed him and grabbed his shoulder.

"Derain! Derain, you said that you saw Sam with those troops on Zangspur?" he asked breathlessly.

Derain gave him a look and shrugged his shoulder free, "I told you I did."

Anton dropped his hand, thought furiously a moment, said "Thanks!" and took off back to the lift.

"That is one strange man," Derain muttered as he headed back to the lounge.

***

Captain Kaplean listened stoically in his ready room as Doctor Wyeth berated him about the loss of her pet genorg. Reports had come back from Chief Bull's team and there was very little debris from the last position the freighter had occupied before it disappeared.

He still waited on his people to gather any intel, even what the blasted ship's name was. The reports from the scans during their battle showed a standard capacity cargo ship from an unknown builder. Nothing in the preliminary reports showed that there was anything special about it. Yet it had fired military ordinance, cloaked and then disappeared through a tear in space.

The ordinance and cloaking device most likely came from the ship that had been left floating in this system. Its designation was M25 though he still waited for confirmation on this.

The way the trawler disappeared didn't have such a readily available explanation.

Either this meant that the ship had been absorbed into some horrifying 'other space' or it had some form of jump capability. Either answer was unsettling.

"Captain! Are you listening to me?" yelled the Doctor. "Captain!"

"Of course, Doctor Wyeth," he replied. "We are doing all that we can to track your genorg, but we are operating under a severe lack of knowledge." His tone darkened as he explained the same thing for what felt like the hundredth time, "We don't recognize the make of that ship. We don't have its name or who captains it. All the travel records for that vessel have been wiped, in two separate systems. Never mind that we don't know if the damn ship even still exists!" He stood up, "Now, if you'll excuse me, I must check on the repairs to my ship so that we will be ready if and when we have a lead."

Doctor Wyeth stood there flabbergasted as the man left the ready room, "How dare he ignore me? I'll see that he loses this commission. Damn that man!" She stomped out of the ready room on her way back to her cabin.

Captain Kaplean watched the Doctor leave the bridge before he turned to the communications officer, "Lieutenant Hayley, please monitor, discretely, the Doctor's outgoing calls. Keep me informed." He acknowledged the "Sir, yes sir" then continued to peruse the damage report.

***

Anton seated himself on the deck of his cabin. He got as comfortable as he could with the rending din that emanated from the hull... never mind the strange ululating screams that had originated a few hours ago. *'Four more days of this... ugh,'* he thought to himself. He took a deep breath, closed his eyes and tried to dredge his memories of the war.

Even though it felt like ages, he had only left the Matilda five years ago, his time. He rubbed his hand on the deck and he muttered, "Three of those years I spent rotting in a cell. I barely saw anyone. Whatever they want me for must have occurred during the war. But what?"

He thought back to the time he had become aware of the revolution. He'd heard rumors of attacks out on some of the edge worlds, but it had been on Pronov that he first heard a man on a street corner talk about revolution and not get carted off by the local police. The man explained the plight of the less affluent and how the government's policies kept them impoverished.

His speech had captivated Anton. He had always lived to survive for himself and for his friends. To understand that he could actually make a change in the way the worlds worked was heady stuff to consider. It consumed him, this desire to matter, to make a difference. He eventually said his goodbyes and jumped ship on Yevis.

Jon Gray Lang

Recruitment for the revolution was high at this point and getting in wasn't difficult. He moved from small cell to small cell of operatives until someone higher up in the chain noticed him. He received basic weapons and tactics training from the ex-merc, Rosa Keri, and excelled. He had fought for the cause on various outer system worlds until he ended up on Tigron. Tigron, where the revolution ended and all the voices of those involved were silenced.

So what was special about him? Who or what did he know that would make someone want him so badly? They didn't seem to want him dead. The only people he even knew who were still alive from those years were Sam, Rosa and old Jimmy. Did they have something to do with it? They had tried to grab him on Chalman's world and, if Derain was right, again on Zangspur. Sam and Rosa had been a pair forever. His memories spiraled back to Tigron.

Sam had been in charge of the revolutionaries in that so called 'police action.' They had made some impressive headway until the Consortium had resorted to nukes. It all fell apart pretty quickly after that. The last of the people on that world were ravaged by starvation and illness. They had to keep moving to avoid the angry mobs. The Consortium troops trapped on that planet didn't fare much better.

In the end only five of the team had made it to trial and only four of them even lived to be incarcerated; just Sam, Rosa, old Jimmy and me. The Butcher of Timmony Bay had captured them all, but they didn't want her. They were definitely the link, but why? Anton cleared his head and sauntered off to the lounge. Mental reflection was hungry work.

***

      Over the next couple of solar days, the cacophony from the hull kept everyone on edge. Luli had tried to play music, but was continually drowned out by the noise. Barney had disappeared into the bowels of the Matilda and no one could find him. Derain had built blockades at the airlock hatches throughout the ship but Jacquie had taken to knocking them over in bouts of frustration. No one slept. Everyone walked around fully armed. The mental stability of the people on board was eroding quickly. Eventually one of them collapsed.

      Jacquie and Luli dragged Mr. Leon down to sickbay and ran him through the scanner, but Doc couldn't find anything wrong. His brain activity initially had rated higher than average, but it had dropped below the normal human range and now he looked the worse for it. When he was conscious, which was becoming exceedingly rare, he could barely form cohesive sentences. As the latest scan completed, Derain burst in on them clutching a fistful of mazuma.

      "That guy brought tons of this on

board! And I finally figured out how he got on the Matilda, too.   He had a sleeper tube hidden underneath everything. In it I found these!" He beamed triumphantly. In Derain's hand was a tube filled with bags of blue dust. "I don't recognize this drug though, do you? How about you Doc?"

"Eee chu tae dom sah," Doc replied.

Luli barked out a laugh before she grabbed the tube from his hands and tore open a packet. She ran some of the fine dust into the molecular scanner. "Just scan it you rusty bag of bolts!"

Doc replied, "Li do sat ae ehhh."

"Who am I to talk? Why you..." Luli hissed through her gritted teeth.

Derain looked at Mr. Leon as he lay forlornly on the examination table and turned to Jacquie, "Think we should put him back in his sleeper? He doesn't look good."

Jacquie walked slowly over to his body.   "Let's get him in there while the two computers here battle it out."

***

Luli burst into laughter when Barney entered the lounge that evening. He was in his space suit and wore the biggest set of headphones any of them had seen. He walked on by as if he couldn't hear a thing and if truth be told, he probably couldn't. Strangely, the screams and gnawing sounds had dissipated over the last hour. The crew wondered if some of the creatures had detached from the hull.

Jacquie caught Barney's eye and mimicked pulling the headphones off. He stopped and stared, grunted then pulled them off.

"It's not as loud!" he shouted.

Jacquie grimaced, "It's not. No need to shout."

"Huh. That can't be good."

Galena came in through the hatch behind him enveloped in space suits. Everyone stared at her as she dropped a suit onto each one of them. "Where's our guest?"

Derain shook himself before he replied, "We put him back in the sleeper tube he used to smuggle himself aboard."

Galena put her hands on her hips and gave a satisfied look, "Well that's good. He'll probably outlive the rest of us." She stepped into her suit.

Luli piped up, "Outlive us?"

"Yes. Those things are preparing to charge us. Barney and I figure they've searched for the weakest points on the hull to get inside the Matilda... to get to us. They've been at it since we arrived and we think they must've chosen their entry point." She pulled the collar up and set the helmet to the shoulder clips, "I'd suggest putting those on. Once they break in, we'll bleed atmo and it'll just be your lungs and whatever is out there." She looked around, "Man, am I hungry.   What did Anton make?"

Anton came into the lounge to find Jacquie, Luli and Derain in various stages of dress. "I see you got the message. Tonight is our Last Supper, as it were. I prepared the best of what we have, just in case." With Galena's help, he set the table and brought out the dishes.

It took a while for everyone to compose themselves and sit down for the evening meal. Conversations ranged from old stories and anecdotes to just about anything to keep their minds off what horrors the near future might hold.

"Luli, did you ever discover what that drug was?" asked Derain.

"Doc thinks it's designed to interact with the mental capacity of a living being, to increase analytical thought processes. It does seem to have a side effect that he couldn't evaluate. No idea why Mr. Leon would need it," she shrugged around her eating. "If it stays this quiet, maybe I'll play a song or three."

Dinner wound down and the galley was put to rights in the relative quiet of the moment... the calm before the storm. Luli pulled out her ukulele and played a handful of tunes while Jacquie worked on a plan to get everyone out of this situation alive.

She called Barney and Derain over to her. Luli stopped playing and joined the rest of the group. Jacquie met the eyes of each crewmember, savoring what might be the last quiet moment she would share with the people she cared about the most. She frowned briefly, "Okay folks, it's like this. We only have to survive out here another day before the ship auto jumps back into our space. We have a timeline and this gives us some options."

Anton bemoaned, "Options? What sort of options? I was on board that wreck. I saw what those things did to that crew. They were a highly trained military team and they were ripped to shreds." He stood up abruptly, "How are we, a dysfunctional group of six partially trained people, supposed to survive what a highly trained team of a hundred people couldn't?"

"Well," Derain offered, "we did cause them all sorts of grief at the same time, and to be honest, they weren't prepared."

"Prepared? How can you prepare for those things?" Anton shouted as he pointed out the viewport.

"Rabbit! Calm!" commanded the Captain. "That's what we're discussing right now.

Anton sat down and Luli put her hand on his arm until he regained his self-control.

"Okay Barney. Tell them what you told me," said Jacquie.

Barney unclenched his hands as he stood up and pulled a schematic of the ship up onto the data table. "From what the Lieutenant and I could tell, the beasts narrowed their attacks to the airlocks. If she is right about a concerted attack, these would be their entry points. The hangar bay and cargo bay doors did attract some attention, but the airlocks seemed to be their main focus." He pointed at the schematic, "I've already sealed the main shaft at both ends, hopefully to keep them out of the engine room. So, we only have two problems: the airlock in the cargo bay and the one off the hangar bay."

Jacquie spoke up at this point, "The plan we've come up with is to barricade the top deck airlock and open the one in the cargo bay."

"What kind of madness is that?" yelled Anton.

Luli uneasily followed with, "We're going to let them in?"

Galena looked at the schematic a moment before she proclaimed, "Aah... Minimize damage to the Matilda. This will allow us to keep an atmosphere in the ship when we break into normal space." She glanced at Jacquie, "Smart."

"This is the plan?" retorted Anton. "We're screwed!"

"Be that as it may be, this is our best chance of survival... long term survival. We need to clear the cargo bay of anything volatile and set up a kill zone," Jacquie said quietly. "So, are we in agreement?" She waited for the nods, reticent as they were in some cases. "Let's get to work."

Anton stood up and walked off toward the hatch, "We are so dead."

Luli looked over at Jacquie, "He's

probably right, you know."

"He probably is, but what else can we do?"

***

The crew met in the cargo bay and began clearing anything that might be dangerous to the sickbay. Doc's protestations were ignored. Everything else was used to form a channel or kill zone from the airlock doors to their defensive position. Even the Rabbit's Folly was turned into a wall for this last ditch affair.

The channel that had been created ran close to the height of the airlock. A shelter was set up at the other end of this funnel and their weapons were arrayed out in an easy to grab fashion. Barney set up a couple of automatic weapon pods at the corners and Derain pulled out an old shoulder launch missile from the crate he had dragged into the room.

"Last resorts, right?" he said half-jokingly.

Once the bay had been as prepared as best it could be, the Captain ordered everyone to get some sleep. No one wanted to be alone, so they puttered about the cargo bay until they collapsed where they stood. Jacquie had waited until everyone else had fallen asleep before she closed her eyes. It struck her that she felt closer to these people, her family, at this very moment, than she'd ever felt before. There was something comforting about having everyone close... something familiar...

"Something familiar..." Galena woke with a start. The hull echoed with the clawing and chittering from the creatures that worked to get at them. "Something about that sound..." She looked around, spied the crew scattered about in all manner of poses of unconsciousness, but her mind stayed preoccupied with the echoes, "It's gotten louder." She searched until she came across Jacquie's sleeping form. She checked her timer, "Only a few hours left. No time like the present."

She shook her awake. "Captain? I think we're close."

Jacquie sat there a moment as she cleared her eyes, "No time like the present, right?" The two ladies gave a small desperate laugh and set about waking the rest of the team.

The time it took to bleed the atmosphere in the cargo bay back into the tanks seemed to pass much too quickly. The racket that came from the hull increased and the bare nerves of the crew reverberated in response. The helmet locks had been closed and everyone had taken up positions for the inevitable.

"Everyone ready?" asked Jacquie.

"Said my last words this morning," Barney retorted.

Luli smirked, "A bit final sounding wouldn't you say?"

"Outer lock opening now," Jacquie

announced. "Overriding inner lock now."

The alarms sounded as both the inner and outer airlock doors opened at the same time. There was a small pop as the last remnants of the internal atmosphere rushed out to be replaced with...

"Ugh. The smell is even worse out there!" Anton fumed.

The sickly bright umber like light from the outside slowly bled into the interior of the cargo bay like a thin fog. The light left a haziness in everyone's vision and a greasiness settled on everything the light touched. The chittering outside the Matilda changed pitch. The hull resonated with the tumult of bodies as the monsters scurried toward the open airlock.

An amorphous blob appeared at the edge of the outer airlock to be followed by something that resembled a stick with thousands of legs. Hooting echoed in the cargo bay intermixed with chittering as more and more creatures from nightmares piled around the airlock.

"Fire!" shouted the Captain.

Derain flipped the propulsion switch on the shoulder mounted launcher and a rocket screamed out of the tube. He grabbed another of the two remaining missiles from the crate and jammed it into the breach. The rocket flew out past the airlocks to detonate among the beasts that floated horrifically against the turmoil of the sky that spun behind them. The explosion tore the tightly packed monsters to pieces and a glistening ichor blossomed outward.

The screams of the beasts were maddening. Their polarized cacophony shattered the silence of space. As the hooting and chittering took on a frenetic tone, a feeding frenzy began outside in that 'other space'. The crew watched in horror as the living beasts tore into the dead and dying ones. Some creatures were devoured whole. The monsters attacked each other until the ichor blocked the sky.

"Derain, fire again!" she ordered.

The second rocket hurled from the tube to explode among the congregation outside. More of the creatures were shredded, but this only escalated their bloodlust. The beasts on the outer edges of the massacre refocused on the open airlock. A swarm of the monsters crawled, slithered and clawed their way into the airlock.

The rattle of gunfire that erupted inside the Matilda drowned out the screeches of the wounded monstrosities. The stench from the dead and dying creatures was beyond comprehension. Anton retched in his helmet. Luli simply disengaged her olfactory senses. But the abominations kept coming.

Anton ran out of ammunition first; he grabbed the next weapon closest to him and fired anew. Barney's auto guns spun with empty, overheated barrels while Galena snagged another rifle. The beasts were making headway into the cargo bay. As they advanced, they crushed the corpses of their kind under their appendages. But it didn't slow their progress. There were just too many of them.

A mob of creatures clambered over the makeshift walls and fell to the other side. Others pressed against the windows of the sickbay until the plas-glass shattered from the pressure. Anton swung around to cover their flank, but it didn't matter... it was too little, too late. Beasts raged as they flew into the cargo bay above the makeshift walls to crash into the decking behind the crew. Rounds fired by the crew became more sporadic and less concentrated as the ammunition dried up.

Everything seemed to slow down for Jacquie. Out of the corner of her eye she watched as Luli's movements accelerated to become more machine-like. She stood transfixed as the cyborg pummeled a creature against the broken sickbay window with inhuman alacrity. Barney was thrown across the cargo bay to rebound against a water tank. He lay still. Derain was pinned against their makeshift barricade with a rifle wedged in front of him. A monster snapped at him, but couldn't get around the obstruction. Jacquie pulled up her pistol and shot the beast multiple times until the gun repeatedly clicked on empty chamber after empty chamber.

She turned as Galena screamed and leapt into the fray of what had been their kill zone, the decking slick underneath her feet. The Lieutenant's empty pistol clattered to the deck. She pulled a knife as she landed on one of the wormlike creatures. It hooted in response and tried to roll over onto her. An octopodal appendage knocked the breath out of the Captain as her head slammed into the decking. Part of her brain kept an eye on Galena as she repeatedly stabbed the monster, her face plate oily with the beast's blood.

"Looks like Rabbit was right after all..." Jacquie mumbled to herself. "But what else could we do? So close, too."

The wormlike beast shook off the Lieutenant and lunged after her as she crashed into the wall. She picked herself up to challenge it. Then suddenly, the timbre of the monster's hoots changed as it caught her scent through her torn suit. Others of the creatures turned to it and warbled in response. The crew watched in amazement as the wormlike thing stretched straight into the air while the Lieutenant, looking tiny in comparison, stood in front of it. It emitted a bizarre ululating roar and the other creatures followed suit.

Just then, the Matilda began its jump back into home space. The ship twisted into itself and the creatures shrieked as they disintegrated right before the eyes of the astonished crew. Barney broke into laughter punctuated by coughs as the Matilda slammed into normal space so violently it knocked Galena off her feet. The blackness of space appeared in the open airlock and the only sound that rivaled Barney's laughing on the open comm channel was the ship's alarm. Jacquie slowly

Jon Gray Lang

got to her feet. She closed the outer airlock door and then the inner one.

Derain began to laugh and Jacquie, who couldn't help herself, joined him. Luli and Anton chimed in while Galena just looked on, perplexed. This prompted another rush of laughter. Luli shushed everyone on the open comm channel.

"I think we're getting some chatter," she interrupted.

A woman's voice came over the comm, "... please respond. Matilda, this is Copperhead, please respond."

Luli stood up and brushed herself off, "I'm on my way topside."

Barney pushed himself to his feet, "I'll check for leaks before we pump atmo back in here."

Jacquie walked over and grabbed the first container and moved it back to where it had been tied down earlier. Anton and Derain slowly followed suit and Galena joined them. Barney walked around the cargo bay with his data pad in hand. He eventually made a full circuit and gave a nod to the Captain. She walked over and started the process that would bring breathable air back into the cargo bay.

"We lucked out on that lunatic plan, Captain," he said.

"I know," she replied. "But, all in all, it was worth it just to prove Anton wrong."

"Ha! Yes, I bet it was," he barked.

"Ugh. Look at all this broken plas-glass," he pointed at the shattered windows around the sickbay. "I don't even want to know what the outer hull looks like."

"You and me both. But Matilda got us through it again, didn't she?" she remarked as she patted the bulkhead.

Barney nodded, "Aye, she did. Just barely this time, but she did."

Luli's voice rang out over the comm, "Hey Jacq, this lady wants to speak with you concerning our delivery."

"On my way up." She turned to those left in the bay, "See what else we need to take care of right now. After that, everyone take a break. It's been a busy day."

Derain piped in, "We lost some food rations, but most of the trash blew out the open airlock. Pretty easy clean up considering."

"Yep. Just another day in paradise," Anton muttered.

twenty-seven

The New Order

Captain Ariel Kahn brought her ship, the Copperhead, around to link up with the Matilda's cargo bay airlock. The sudden appearance of the craft had set off proximity alarms on board her vessel, never mind the stress on her crew. After her spotlights played over the hull of the Matilda, she didn't want to know what it had survived.

The deep rents in the hull, as if some large clawed beast had tried to tear the boat open, caught her eyes. It was like something from the old spacer's stories. It gave her the creeps.

Her liaison at the jump gate hadn't received a manifest from the Spur system, so the arrival had been a complete surprise. The ship out there gave the correct call sign for the pickup, but even their employer had become concerned with the lack of any travel mandates for the Matilda. He had even lost contact with his representative on board back in the Spur system.

But here it was and she had no idea how it had gotten here. It wasn't much bigger than the Copperhead, but it definitely had not come through unscathed. The engines had been blasted apart; the hull was covered in gouges and quite a bit of flotsam floated around the airlock her ship attempted to link to. She kept watch as her tunnel extended out and connected to the airlock. She registered the clear connection response from her crewman, Hancock.

"Boarding team, meet me at the lock." She turned to face her companion, "Are you coming Mr. Leon?"

***

Luli decided to come down to the cargo bay for the meeting. Where else was there to be? She received a brisk nod from Jacquie, but could feel how on edge everyone was. There was no escape available. However this played out, they wouldn't be able to run. They were almost out of ammunition and everyone was exhausted. All of Mr. Leon's goods that remained on board, which included his tube, were stacked neatly in the middle of the cargo bay. The temperature of the bay was still cold as it had not yet normalized. It was still a mess.

Jon Gray Lang

***

Captain Kahn waited politely until the inner air lock opened before her. As it did, her senses were assaulted by an incredibly nauseous odor. She coughed loudly and leaned her left hand against the bulkhead, then immediately jerked back from whatever squelched under her fingers. The viscous black fluid clung to her fingers as she vigorously wiped her hand against her pant leg. The material was sprayed all over the air lock entrance.

Jacquie strode forward to shake her hand, "Captain Jacquotte Delahaye of the Matilda. She's usually in better shape than this, but it's been a tough week. Welcome aboard."

"Uh, thank you Captain. Captain Ariel Kahn at your service." She kept wiping at her hand.

Jacquie pointed to the pile of goods stacked neatly in the middle of what could only be called a disaster site. "Here are the goods as promised. Our benefactor is in the sleeper's tube." Her eyes widened as Mr. Leon stepped in behind the boarding crew of the Copperhead.

Anton's voice echoed loudly in the cargo bay, "How many of you are there?"

Ariel turned at the dry laughter that came from Mr. Leon. He smirked, "Didn't he tell you? We are many and we are one." He strode forward to shake the hand of Captain Delahaye,

"Thank you for delivering my shipment. I do appreciate your timely arrival and your discretion in this matter." He turned to Captain Kahn, "If you please."

Ariel waved her people forward to load the crates on board the Copperhead. She kept an eye on her employer while he spoke to this other Captain as if they were party to some shared secret. He laughed as he patted Ms. Delahaye on the back before he turned back toward her.

"Captain? Please have your engineers work with the Titan fellow over there to commence repairs on this ship." He studied her displeased expression, "I may have need of it soon."

Ariel keyed her comm to call her engineering team to come over. She turned to Mr. Leon, "All parts on board my ship are at the Matilda's disposal?"

"That is correct, Captain." He gave her a half-hearted smile, "Do not worry. Your inventory will be replaced." Her relief was palpable as her demeanor changed. "Please have this tube placed in my cabin. I prefer it to be left undisturbed. I am feeling a bit peckish. I believe I will grab a bite to eat. Captain Delahaye, would you care to join me? "

Jacquie looked at Mr. Leon and back at Ms. Kahn. She walked slowly over to Ariel, "Permission to come aboard, Captain?"

"Permission granted, Captain." Ariel relaxed within the confines of formality. "It's good to meet someone who knows the proper procedures. Thank you." She turned back to her employer, "I will oversee your cargo transfer, sir. Now, if you will excuse me?"

***

Mr. Leon waved Jacquie toward the airlock and the two of them entered the tunnel to the Copperhead. "She always gets a bit piqued when she doesn't know all the details."

"I can understand. I feel the same way," returned Jacquie. "I'll have to give her a huge thanks for getting my boat up and running. Did you know my ship was going to need repairs? And, are we also going to discuss payment for this rather clandestine delivery over lunch?"

"Of course, of course. I just need to finalize a few points with my compatriot. You know... find out exactly what was offered and so forth," he winked.

"Your, uh, compatriot, as you call him, got pretty sick during our travels. We did what we could for him, but as I'm sure you've noticed, other things came up," she rejoined thinly.

"Oh yes. It looks to have been quite exciting. You must tell me all about it," he responded pleasantly.

***

Jon Gray Lang

"Are you the Titan?" a woman asked Barney.

He gave her and her companion a once over, "Do you see anyone else about with such an impressive stature?"

"Uh, my apologies," she said flustered. "I am Helena Thielle and this is my assistant, Myles Falvella. We're here to help out, if you need it."

"I'll take whatever help I can get. Just look around. Fix what you can." He rubbed his hands over his face, "I'll be outside checking on my engines."

"Oh! We have a preliminary report from our scans concerning your engines!" piped up Myles.

"Aah, I like you already, lad," smiled Barney.

***

Anton set the crate down with the help of Derain. "That looks to be the last of the undamaged ones; just broken bits are left." He looked conspiratorially at the bounty hunter, "Hey, what do you know about that guy... or guys, I guess?"

"Just what everyone knows. He's a powerful member of the syndicate and has a dangerous reputation. No one messes with him and he seems to be everywhere at once. But I think we've figured out why that is." He glanced at Anton,

"Why? What's up?"

"Nothing much; I just don't trust him."

"You don't trust him?" Derain responded incredulously. "Hell, I don't trust you."

Anton glanced around a moment before he locked eyes with Derain, "Look. I know I haven't done much except cause trouble since you guys yanked me off that prison ship. But I think somebody wants me, because of Sam. If you were right about seeing him on Zangspur, then I'm pretty sure he is the reason for why we keep getting hassled. I just don't know how or why."

"You're going to ask me for help, aren't you?" Derain glared. "Help me get the Resonator set up and then you can ask me."

"Sure. Fine." Anton followed him over to the Resonator, a simple cleaning device that essentially shook the filth off the walls and decks with sound waves. If the correct ear protection wasn't worn, though, it could cause permanent hearing damage to a person.

"We're going to run the Resonator for a bit. Make sure to protect your ears," Derain shouted to the whole bay. He waited until he got affirmatives from everyone. "Rabbit, channel seven."

The Resonator kicked on and Derain played the shaft along the cargo bay walls. Where the sound waves hit, the crusted ichor exploded into dust and fell to the deck. He moved methodically from one wall to the next one. Those who were in the cargo bay moved away from him as Anton fed him more piping for greater distance.

Derain looked up, "Even on the ceiling? "By the Major" as Lu would say." He snaked out the piping until the crusted ichor rained down around him. "Face away from everyone when you talk, Okay Rabbit? We don't know if any of these people are lip readers. Now what were you going to ask me?"

Anton turned toward the wall behind the Resonator, "I feel like an idiot talking to a wall."

"You are an idiot..."

Anton ignored the insult and interrupted, "You've got sources, right? I was thinking maybe you could find out more about Sam. I have to figure out why he would be after me and..."

"...who is financing him?" Derain interjected. "Got it. Best idea you've had all day. Now, what do I get out of this deal if I decide to help you?"

"Besides not randomly having to fear for your life at a moment's notice?"

"Yeah, besides that."

Anton shrugged, "I don't have much. What would you want?"

Derain thought for a moment, "A favor. A favor from you at some later date."

"A future promise? Alright, done," Anton agreed.

Satisfied, Derain finished with,

"Excellent. Our deal is made. And with that, I believe our work here is done, too. Kill the machine."

Anton switched the Resonator off and rolled up the piping. As Derain announced the job was done, an audible sigh of relief came from the others in the cargo bay. Derain walked up to Anton and extended his hand. Anton stared a bit before he shook it. "What have I just signed myself on for?" he wondered.

***

"From what your scans show, I'm down one engine," Barney grumbled.

"You should be able to scavenge it for parts," said Helena. She pulled up her inventory list, "It looks like we can replace the guts on the burned one with what we have on hand. It's a different make, but there should be room in the housing."

Barney perked up, "Similar input/output levels?"

"It's more powerful, but the energy drain should be less. Hmm..." she pondered for a moment.

Myles pointed at something on her data pad from behind her, "Aha! Your engine set up is a little strange, but I believe we can augment it to be roughly on par with the newer one we'd install."

"I think I am in love with you both!" Barney gave her a big smile then flashed another toothy grin at Myles. Both of the engineers from the Copperhead blushed.

***

The two ships remained locked together in this blank point of space for almost two weeks, ship time. On board the Matilda, the armory stores had been replenished to a point that if a fight was provoked, they wouldn't need to run from it. Repairs proceeded at a decent pace, and according to the engineers, sublight propulsion would be up and running soon. The structural damage to the outside of the ship was mostly cosmetic. "Thank goodness for heavy armor," Luli had declared.

Over time, the two crews had blended in cooperation and comradery. They shared meals and swapped stories. And as work sessions ended bawdy songs and laughter rang throughout the two ships. The two Captains relaxed and commiserated over a bottle of the 'good stuff'. It was a pleasant respite, but Jacquie was itching to get under way.

***

Mr. Leon entered his cabin to find the sleeper tube open and the other Mr. Leon on the edge of his bed. "I came as soon as I was able. It is good to see that you are well."

"It is good to see another of my brethren after so long a stint abroad."

"It is also good to see you returned to the fold. May I ask what happened? The Captain of the Matilda was good enough to give me the tale of woe on Zangspur."

"Yes, a terrible loss that. But information gained. The operation can be rebuilt there, given time."

"Time and resources. We lost connection with you during your stay aboard the Matilda. The loss affected you in an unexpected way?"

"Yes, quite unexpected. That freighter has some form of jump capability unknown to us. In the sudden transition it separated me from the fold. The consequences were unexpected."

"Jump capability you say? Oh, that is quite useful information."

"I thought you might be pleased."

"This plays well with the next stage, doesn't it?"

"Oh, quite."

The two Mr. Leon's nodded to each other and the one that had sat on the edge of the bed exited the cabin. The other sat bemusedly on one end of the sleeper tube, "Wonderful when the pieces come together, isn't it?"

twenty-eight

Two Against One

Days later, the Matilda was able to move under its own propulsion once again. The engineers had celebrated fiercely and the price for that, come morning, would be high. Jacquie chuckled as she stepped off the lift onto the second deck of her ship. It would feel wonderful to soon be underway. She didn't have a set direction as of yet, but Mr. Leon had come through and their pay had made a tidy sum.

Of course, some of that mazuma went to Captain Kahn as they had raided her inventory. However, their benefactor had covered some of those costs as well. Both ships would go their separate ways in the hypothetical morning. As a personal thank you, Jacquie had given her second to last bottle of real whisky to the Captain of the

Copperhead. She had saved that one for a special occasion, but to be alive and still have a working boat was special enough. Lost in her own thoughts, she almost trampled the strangely silent Mr. Leon as he stood outside the gym hatch.

"Good evening, Captain. I trust all is well?" he inquired.

She jumped back shocked, "Oh! Hello... uh, yes, everything does seem to be moving along fine." She stopped, flustered, "How are you?"

He moved to her left side, "I am doing quite well. Tell me Captain, have you chosen a destination as of yet?"

"That very thought has been occupying my mind this very night."

Mr. Leon put on a dour face, "I do hope you have taken into account that your ship might have been recognized from that mess in the Spur system. Your use of the jump gate out of this system may end up being used to track you."

"It's one of the angles I have taken into account. The only plus would be that it would take the Consortium quite a bit of time to track us out to the Luthien system." She made a wry face, "My wonder is why did you choose this particular system to rendezvous in?"

He chuckled, "It is of no consequence. Luthien is known amongst smugglers like yourself as an excellent drop off point. No real law to speak of and the Consortium turns a blind eye. Sometimes it is a very expensive eye, but it turns none the less."

"Convenience, then. That I can understand." She opened the hatch to the gym, "I'm going to blow off some energy. Want to join me?"

He walked in after her, "I would like to continue our conversation, so yes, I will join you."

He followed her over to the weight set. She set it to her liking before she turned to him, "Excellent. You can spot me. It'll keep Mr. de Lagnel from blowing a gasket." She laughed at his mild surprise.

He watched her as she went through her routine. They traded places and she watched him go through his.

"All these questions make me wonder if you're driving to some point," she said. "Now, as a ship's captain, known for hauling cargo and a dalliance with smuggling, this makes me wonder if you might have a job to offer me?"

He finished his reps and they switched positions again. "Actually, I did have a proposition for you and your crew. In fact, I think it may even stall the search for your ship."

"Oh, really?" Wouldn't that be convenient?" Jacquie smirked.

"It is a concept you have a solid grasp of, I hear," he joked.

The two of them traded places once again. Mr. Leon looked up at her as he continued, "I have a particularly profitable delivery, but it needs to be kept secret. As no one knows that you are here, you jumped to the top of my list."

"So secrecy is covered, but what else could possibly set us apart from, say your ship the Copperhead? She has a capable captain and she is a good vessel." She gave him a grin.

He smiled back as he continued, "I have need of her elsewhere. Besides, you've proven that your crew can handle all sorts of situations." He watched her stare at him as if trying to peel back the layers. "Of course," he continued, "the fact that your freighter has jump capability also pushed you to the top of my list."

"Aah. I was wondering if you were our Mr. Leon." She put her finger to her mouth, "But, with the government after us, this does seem a rather dangerous proposition."

"That's the beauty of it, though. This is a government contract." He gave her an infectious grin.

Jacquie erupted in peals of laughter. As he put the bar down, she leaned on his hands and gave him a leer, "Oh, you are a tricky one, Mr. Leon. Though, if we are to continue working together, you will need a first name. I detest formality." She put her finger to her mouth once again, "And I think I have the perfect one." She pushed off the bar and helped him up, "From now on, I will call you Rex."

***

Upon the rise of the sun used by the

Consortium to track time, traffic between the two ships hit a fever pitch. Multiple crates were being shuffled from the Copperhead to the Matilda. Barney supervised the attachment of two shipping containers to the Matilda and locked them in place. While the Copperhead looked to be a smaller ship, it still carried a couple of containers.

As is the formal way of ship to ship meetings, the two crews met at the airlock and wished each other luck in their endeavors. The tunnel was retracted and the crew of the Matilda watched as the Copperhead peeled off and disappeared into the darkness.

Barney turned to the Captain, "Repairs are as complete as they can be. We can travel under our own power again. I am even of the opinion that our shiny, new cloak will not thoroughly drain the ship's power."

Galena waited until he finished, "The ship is also ready for battle if need be."

"My ship is ready to roll, too," stated Derain. "We have work, I assume?"

Luli spoke up, "We sure do. Everybody prep for a jump to the Pequiz system. We're off to Ninguiz in less than five minutes."

Over the groans, Anton announced, "Breakfast will be served in ten minutes. I was able to trade for some nice eggs."

Jacquie looked proudly at her crew; her family. They had just slogged through a pile-of-awful, yet they still stood with her. "Alright, people, this is a short jump. So, let's get the hell out of here!"

***

The Matilda folded into itself as it disappeared into a red, lightning filled bubble in space. After a relatively uneventful trek, compared to their previous journey through the 'other space', she reappeared in the Pequiz system... a system that was currently cluttered with ships of every shape and size on their way to escape the system through the jump gate.

"Whoa!" yelled Luli as she pulled the Matilda off its axis. "Barney! Give the engines more juice! It's like a traffic jam out here!"

Derain stared at the comm, "What is going on? All these ships are just flashing their transponders. I can't get an answer from any of them."

"Jacquie, I am getting some strange gravitational flux! It's playing havoc with the ship!" Luli barked.

"What the hell are you doing up there, Lu?" Barney's voice boomed over the comm. "I'm getting tossed about back here!"

Galena's eyes shifted from her weapons station to the bow port. She could just make out the planet Ninguiz against the star of this system. She glanced over and noticed that Anton was doing the same thing.

Derain stated, "Captain, I'm getting a beacon response from the system jump gate. Full evacuation protocol has been called. What is going on out here?"

"That's what I need you to find out, Derain, and the sooner the better," Jacquie ordered. "Luli, time to destination?"

Luli scanned through her navigation trajectory, "At this rate, only a couple hours for us. Jeez! Who is flying those wrecks?"

Anton spoke slowly and with dread, "I don't think anyone is flying those wrecks, Lu. I think those are ghost ships."

"Damn it! Madness!" growled Luli.

Jacquie looked quizzically at Anton, "Ghost ships?"

"During the war on Tigron, full evacuation protocol was in effect. Refugees attempted to get off planet in anything that could fly, but pilots were at a shortage then. Some unscrupulous types would take the refugee's currency; program a ship's computer to rendezvous at the jump gate and promise escape from the system." He ruminated, "If the Consortium has declared full evacuation protocol, there's a good bet that the jump gate is no longer manned."

"Better to get off planet and out through the gate though, right?" she asked.

His sad eyes pierced hers, "If the calculation to the gate is off at all, even one arcsecond, that ship will just sail past the jump gate altogether. It'll fly out into unknown space, never to be heard from again." He rubbed his hand across his face, "There were a lot of Tigron ships that were never recovered... just gone."

Jacquie didn't want to imagine how badly it went for those refugees. They would either kill each other for food and water or freeze to death as the ship burned through its power. Her body shivered at the thought. "But how can there be a war and there's no news about it?"

Anton just stared at her.

The next hour and a half passed quietly for the crew. The flight of ships lessened, but there were many that were already floating dead. They'd had enough power to get off world before the engines cut out, but no more than that. The planet of Ninguiz grew larger in the bow port, and the mood on the ship grew somber.

"Is there something on the other side of that mud ball?" Luli asked before she changed their angle of trajectory to the planet. A dark corona glimmered just around the edge of the orb. Luli altered their approach just a hair more to be able to see what was on the other side.

As the ship entered orbit around Ninguiz, everyone stared in shock at the center of the corona. Anton muttered out loud in disbelief, "What the hell is that?"

twenty-nine

Lead Sails (and a Paper Anchor)

Purplish black light pulsated wildly within the enormous fissure that tore through the night sky. The Consortium fleet parked between it and the planet was illuminated by the sickly light as it played along the hulls of the vessels. Explosions rocked the heavens and ships burned briefly in the blackness as a battle raged between the fleet and a ragged collection of ships.

These other craft either floated or rocketed back and forth into the slit while a much larger ship was trapped within it. Shadows of darkness greater than the blackness of space slithered and lapped against the sides of the large vessel and kept it from slipping free. The crew of the Matilda looked on, aghast.

"Derain," Jacquie whispered as she

pulled her eyes away from the bow port, "See about getting that call sign up that Mr. Leon gave us. I want to drop this cargo and get the hell out of here."

"Call sign Odin now broadcasting, Captain."

Anton stared in horror at the rift, "Didn't we just leave that place? That looks a lot like where the Matilda goes when we jump." He turned to look at the other crew members, "Am I right?"

Luli responded, "It gives off similar energy readings. Higher levels, but similar." She keyed the comm to the engine room, "Barney! You should come up and see this." She toggled a few switches, "I'm recording these readings, Jacq."

A smaller ship attacked a Consortium destroyer only to detonate as the Matilda moved inexorably closer to the battle. The government fleet appeared to have the edge as the other ships showed heavy damage. Radio chatter on multiple channels siphoned through the comm as the Odin call sign was broadcast.

"Odin? Odin? Please respond," came through the comm.

Derain locked out the other channels. "This is Odin. Is this Zeus? Repeat. Is this Zeus?"

"...Please respond. Odin! This is Zeus."

"We are receiving you, Zeus. What is the trajectory?"

"Head toward coordinates 902-

mark-5, ship designation CBC Remus."

"A battle cruiser? Mr. Leon wasn't lying about this being a government contract," muttered Anton.

Luli responded, "I've got us locked in. You sure about this, Jacq? This is not our usual customer, so to speak."

"Sure as I can be. Everyone, play this safe. Keep weapons visible, but ready. Luli, you stay up top in case we need to leave in a hurry. Derain, take over the weapons station. Galena? Anton? With me."

As they stepped past Barney on his way onto the bridge, they heard him utter, "What in the nine hells?"

The journey to the CBC Remus went smoothly, even though it was punctuated with small explosions from the excitement around them. The Consortium Battle Cruiser Remus had concentrated its fire against the large ship trapped in the void but it was to no avail. Each missile that was launched at the ship disappeared into the rift and the vessel remained stable. It hung there like a question unanswered.

The Matilda pulled up to the battle cruiser, entered the hangar bay and settled onto the decking. Luli's voice rang out over the comm, "We're down. We're in the belly of the beast!"

"Always so melodramatic..." Jacquie whispered under her breath. She stood with Galena and Anton in the cargo bay. Their weapons were out, but held down... just in case. A knock on the airlock punctuated the quiet. Jacquie triggered the airlock open. Moments later, an officer with two guards strolled in.

"Permission to come aboard?" he asked.

Jacquie proclaimed, "Permission granted. Nice bay you've got here." She waited as the officer stepped forward to introduce himself.

"Standard design, I believe; not really my forte. I am Munitions Officer Graeme. And you are...?" He thought furiously, "Oh right, clandestine. Umm, how should I refer to you?"

"Captain always worked for me," Jacquie retorted.

Anton muttered out loud, "Munitions?"

"Well, who else would you expect to pick up this kind of cargo?" Graeme answered somewhat jokingly. He wondered at the lack of response from these people. "Wait. You don't know what your cargo is? Wow."

"We generally operate under a veil of secrecy," Jacquie covered.

"Oh, of course! I just need you to sign here on the delivery of two nuclear warheads. If you please?"

"I am not signing anything."

Anton blurted, "Nuclear warheads?"

Jacquie glared at Anton until he quieted down. "This is a secret shipment. Secret, as in no records. Understood?"

Munitions Officer Graeme stared blankly a moment before he flashed a surprised smile. "My misunderstanding. I'm new to all this cloak and dagger stuff." He keyed his comm, "Okay people, get in here and unload this cargo! Grappling team, get those containers stowed on board!" He turned to Jacquie, "Payment will be brought in momentarily. Captain, if you'll excuse me."

She turned to Galena, "Lieutenant? Head to the shaft to unlock those containers, please." She looked over at Anton, "You. Stay here."

thirty

Corona

Lieutenant Hayley was at her station when a high priority message came through. It was sealed with a Special Operations Informations tag. She dumped it to a chip, wiped the receiving history and eye printed the authorization for its retrieval. She stood up, walked to the captain's station and waited as he signed off on the required daily forms for Yeoman Fitzpatrick. "Sir? New orders." She handed him the chip and walked back to her station, "I wonder where we're off to now?"

The Captain held the chip loosely in his hand as he contemplated it. There had been nothing identifiable from the missing freighter in local space. Nothing like it had shown up on the jump gate reports. No records could be found planet side on Zangspur. For all apparent effect, the ship had disappeared. Moreover, the fact that it effectively had disappeared in front of his crew was not lost on him.

"Helm. You have command," he ordered as he headed to his ready room. Once he sat down, he pushed the chip into the memory slot of his data reader. The chip activated and requested his access code.

"Command Code H-213-57-CDE-7."

The data reader regurgitated the orders that had been sent out a week before from Prime on Jard in the Malina system. He perused the data before he keyed the comm to Doctor Wyeth's cabin.

"Doctor? We have received new orders. The search will have to be canceled in the meantime.

The Doctor's voice came through the comm, "We have not found her, Captain. We cannot leave! I forbid it!"

"Yes, I understand. You can register a complaint. Kaplean out." He keyed the comm off and switched to Navigation, "Grissom? Set a course for the Pequiz system."

thirty-one

Diggin' My Grave

Anton kept watch in the cargo bay as soldiers came through and collected the crates the Matilda had delivered. He felt the decking under his feet shift as one and then the other container were unbolted from the chassis. The battle cruiser was large enough that he didn't feel any effects from the battle that raged on outside. Only a direct hit to it would even make the craft shudder from an impact.

Jacquie's voice came through the comm, "Rabbit, wait for the bounty hunter; then both of you join me out here." She keyed to another private comm channel, "Galena, get top side with Luli. Things are about to go south."

Anton rolled his eyes and grimaced, "Can't anything go smoothly?"

Derain and Anton had just left the

Matilda to stand with Jacquie when an officer, followed by a platoon of Consortium marines, entered the hangar bay of the CBC Remus. The officer held her hands out in supplication, "Captain, I am very sorry, but we need to commandeer your ship."

***

Luli turned to watch Galena as she entered the bridge, "Hey, take the weapons station, would you? A throng of soldiers just showed up outside. I'm hoping we don't have to do a Snatch-n-Bang, but best to be prepared right?"

***

The officer continued, "We can put you on the surface of the planet below or on Jard in the Malina system. The choice is yours."

"Alright people, sometimes I think we lose sight of our objective... if you know what I mean," Jacquie whispered through the comm. She turned to the officer, "And you are...?"

"Objective? What objective?" giggled Luli. "Do you know what she means?"

"I haven't got a clue. Is she talking in code?" Barney pondered wryly over the comm.

"I am Commander Ilya Shafar. Do we have an understanding then?"

Everyone could hear the frustrated

grumble that escaped Jacquie before she cut the comm channel. "Why does everything have to be explained to the last detail?" she asked. Derain just shrugged in return. Anton shuffled his feet into a more anchored stance.

Jacquie glared at the officer, "I can't really allow that to happen, Ilya Shafar. That ship is my life. It's my home. If you try to take her from me, I'll just make her disappear..." She waved her arms, waited a moment, "Disappear..."

"I think she's talking to us, Barney. What could she possibly mean?" Luli deliberated over the comm, with her tongue firmly in her cheek.

Jacquie dropped her arms and Anton smiled as the Matilda simply vanished. Anton glanced over at Derain and mouthed, "Magic trick." Derain pointedly ignored him. The expression of surprise on the marines was palpable.

"Captain, we do not have time for games. If necessary, you won't leave this ship alive... Marines, take aim!" The platoon pulled up and covered the three crew members of the Matilda stranded in the hangar bay.

Jacquie dropped her gaze as if in defeat before she pointedly looked over at the recently unloaded warheads from the containers lying in the bay. She walked up to stare the Commander in the eye, "If I don't leave this ship alive with my people and my freighter, no one will." She pointed toward the warheads.

Jon Gray Lang

***

"That one's for you, Lieutenant." announced Luli.

Galena replied, "Got it.   Target locked."

***

Commander Shafar's face turned gray as she received a request from the bridge of the battle cruiser asking why a weapons targeting system had locked onto something inside the hangar bay.

"Now... you and your men can stand down and let us leave or this conversation is over," Jacquie stated.

The Commander turned away from her, deeply engaged in transmissions over her personal comm. She stepped behind the marines. Jacquie continued to glare at her.

***

A ping bounced off the hull of the Matilda. Luli tracked it to a scanner that was attempting to locate the ship. "Hey Jacquie, they're pinging us. Not sure how the cloak works in regards to that. May want to put a stop to it." She looked over at Galena, "Isn't this fun? I mean who doesn't like to play Chicken?"

"Chicken is a small food bird... right?"

she asked quizzically.

***

"Commander, I will give you until the count of three to decide how today is going to play out. Got it?"

"Marines, stand down. My apologies, Captain." Shafar sidled up to Jacquie, "Let me try to appeal to the merchant in you. The Consortium is willing to buy your ship."

"Not for sale."

"Okay... We're willing to buy your services then. Another delivery?"

"What and where?"

"A small thermo-nuclear device and to that ship out there." Ilya pointed toward where the fissure floated in space. "We have to close that tear in space, but it's anchored to that ship. We've tried to blow it out of the sky, but the ordinance just bypasses the damn thing and goes into the rift instead."

"Not my concern. Just let us go and we all live... simple as that."

"It's not as simple as that! This is the second system we've lost to them. We have to stop them here."

"I am not putting my crew on board that ship. You got that? We don't do suicide missions."

"I'll do it, Captain." Galena stated

over the comm.

"What?" both Luli and Jacquie said at the same time.

"It's true. They have to be stopped here. A stable gateway for those creatures can't be left to exist. Everyone out here would be affected, if we left it open... everyone."

"But it's an impossible job! Those things will tear you to pieces!" sputtered Jacquie.

"They didn't kill me when they got on board. In fact, they backed away from me. Captain, this is a last hope mission. I can do it. I will do it." Galena switched the comm to broadcast in the hangar bay, "This is Lieutenant Galena Chadov. I'll take your deal, if you let the rest of the crew go."

"Lieutenant Chadov? Why does that name sound familiar?" the Commander muttered. She cupped her ear and nodded, "Captain Ellsbeth accepts your deal, Lieutenant. She says the rest of you are free to go."

***

"How do you intend to get over there?" Luli asked her.

Galena thought furiously, "I'm not sure yet. Maybe someone can drop me off?"

***

Jacquie ordered, "Stand down

Lieutenant. Bring her back down, Pilot."

"Yes sir, Captain, sir." Luli disengaged the cloaking device while Galena shut down the targeting system. "Just so you know, Captain, I am saluting. I know you love that stuff," Luli continued.

"Shut it. Lieutenant, we will have a conversation... now." Jacquie turned to Anton and Derain, "Keep an eye on things down here, would you?"

***

Galena waited on the bridge with Luli who remained jacked into the Matilda. Jacquie stomped in through the hatch and glared at the back of Luli's head. Then she turned her glare onto the Lieutenant. Galena relaxed a little once the corner of her eye caught the smirk on Luli's face.

Jacquie keyed her data pad, then held it up and thumped Ms. Qing in the back of the head. Galena squinted; she could barely make out what was written on the screen. But Luli turned and gasped as she read the message on the screen, "We are being recorded," it said. "No names, no IDs. See if you can isolate this room."

Jacquie cleared the pad, exhaled loudly and flopped down in her chair. "What am I going to do with you, Lieutenant? Do you understand what a chain of command is? It means you don't make decisions without my say so. Did you ask for my approval before you made that decision? Did you?"

Luli turned and gave Jacquie a thumbs up, "Bridge is isolated. All channels shut down. They can't hear us, but we can't hear our people either."

You could feel the momentary relief flood from Jacquie, "Thanks, Lu. How long?"

"Their tech is already trying to crack it. Keep it short."

She turned back to Galena, "What the hell are you doing? Broadcasting your name around like that? You are an escaped convict, remember?"

Galena's shoulders straightened as she stared Jacquie down, "I was trained for this and I know it can be done. Don't ask me how I know, I just do. I just need someone to get me over there. You can either help me or let me leave."

"While I commend your sense of duty, my duty is to my crew. Why should we help you? Why should I risk them?"

"I have already explained this!" Galena jumped to her feet and stood at rigid attention before she snapped out a sharp salute, "Permission to leave, Captain?"

"Will you sit down? We need some time to figure this out."

"I can't keep them out much longer, Jacq. It's now-or-never decision time. If it helps, I can get the Lieutenant over there in the Waratah... if Derain will let me borrow her, of course."

"The choice is his, then. If he won't agree, we'll go from there." Jacquie rubbed her face, "With me, Lieutenant."

The ride down the lift and outside to the hangar bay was a quiet one. In the meantime, the crew of the CBC Remus had set up a table surrounded by chairs. Galena stood off to the side as Jacquie approached Derain, "We need to call in a favor."

He quietly pondered what kind of a favor would be needed. Suddenly all of the soldiers in the hangar bay came to attention. "Captain on deck!" rang out. A petite, gray haired woman entered the bay followed by two more guards. She walked over and took a seat at the table across from the crew of the Matilda.

"A bit overkill on the guards, wouldn't you say?" remarked Jacquie as she pulled out a chair for herself.

"Times of war and all, you know." She waved away the platoon. "To put it lightly, threatening to blow up my ship did not engender much trust."

The marines left the hangar as Galena took a seat on one side of Jacquie and Derain sat on the other. Anton stood between the table and their ship. He and the two guards who had accompanied the Captain were the only ones who remained standing in the emptied hangar.

"Pretty motley bunch for a Special Ops team. Cargo hauling and... did my tech hear right?   A bounty hunter?   You must get around. Pretty good cover." She unlinked her hands, "Had me fooled until your Lieutenant there slipped up. These new drone soldiers are so inexperienced. But who am I to judge? You were ordered here and I need the help."

A grimace crossed Anton's face at the suggestion that they were government soldiers.

Jacquie stuttered momentarily before she replied, "We came as soon as we could. What's the situation?"

"As the Commander told you, this system has been invaded by the same unfathomable enemy that took the Leporis system. That system is gone; completely dead. Potune and Rater are barren. Every single citizen of those two worlds are gone. Nothing lives in that system now. We can't afford to let them take this one, too. We'll kill it to keep it out of their hands."

She saw the consternation on the faces of the people around the table and wiped at her brow before she continued, "Let me give you a little bit of history. The proximity alarm went off at this system's jump gate when that fleet appeared out of nowhere over Ninguiz. We were dispatched to deal with the invasion. We kept their ships occupied, but our ground forces took a pounding. We eventually lost contact with the surface all together. That big ship out there is somehow keeping the rift open. The only thing we can think of to close it down is to blow it up. We've sent everything at it and nothing gets near it... on this side. It all disappears into that tear in space. We don't know what happens to the ordinance once it passes through."

She turned to one of her guards, "Harry, a drink please." She waited until he poured her a couple fingers and then she slammed it. "We're all out of small craft that would be able to get a bomb on board that vessel. The last ditch plan is to ram that boat and all hands would go down with the ship, but we also received orders to nuke the planet. I hate to do that to my people down there and up here. So, that's where you come in. You and your ship are my second hope."

Jacquie sat quietly while she ingested the Captain's story. This lady was willing to sacrifice her entire crew and kill everyone left on that mud ball down there to keep this invader from taking it. It was almost too much to take in. Galena displayed the same stone faced expression that Captain Ellsbeth did. Did she understand the need for a decision this extreme? How could she live with it? Her estimation of the Lieutenant changed once again. She held her breath a moment before she exhaled in a whoosh, "D? We're going to need to borrow your ship."

***

Back on board the Matilda, Derain was shouting at Jacquie, "There is no way you're taking my ship into... into that! Do you hear me? No way!"

"Luli would be taking it, not me."

Derain stopped dumbfounded, "You already got her to sign off on this?"

"The Lieutenant did." Jacquie keyed the comm, "How much longer till you're ready to launch, Lu?"

"I need another five minutes, then we're clear."

"Thanks." She keyed the comm to the bridge, "Are we ready to disembark Rabbit?"

"We can meet our illustrious pilot's deadline," he dead panned.

"Jacquie!" Derain shouted, "You can't take my ship without some kind of collateral, damn it!"

Jacquie stopped in her tracks and her head bowed. "If she doesn't return... you can have the Matilda. It's what you really want, isn't it?"

He watched her walk toward the lift as his reply echoed in the now empty hangar bay, "Not this way."

***

Barney worked feverishly with Luli and Galena to get the Waratah set up for this lunatic mission. He and Galena locked the thermonuclear device into its cradle. He stepped back and wiped his hands on his legs. "Are you sure about this, Lu?

I know the Lieutenant here is a flake, but you?"

"She has this deranged theory that the inhabitants of that void are attracted to heat. Not just any heat, but the body heat of a living being." Luli strapped herself into the pilot seat, "As the only cyborg here, I'm the only one who can drop my body temperature and hopefully escape notice. So the crazy lady, who thinks those things don't like her, and I are the only ones who can do it."

Galena stuck her tongue out at Luli. She returned the gesture and Barney just shook his head.

"Go on, Barney. We'll see you on the other side!" Luli smiled.

"That's what concerns me, luv." he muttered.

***

Jacquie clicked the lock on the second personnel carrier that was now attached to her ship. "I do not like having passengers on board." She keyed the comm, "Anton, the carriers are locked. Do we have clearance yet?"

"I still can't believe you're willing to make this pick up, Captain. We all know how much you hate passenger manifests."

"After the look both you and Galena gave me? How could I leave anybody on that rock to die?" answered Jacquie. "On my way up."

Jon Gray Lang

***

"We have clearance in less than three minutes. Better hustle," Anton responded.

Derain shook his head, "I do not like this plan."

"You and me both, buddy," said Anton. "You and me both."

thirty-two

Streets of Laredo

The CBC Remus slowly maneuvered as close to the rift as it dared and let loose a torrent of weapons fire at the remnants of the invading fleet. The hangar bay doors opened and the Matilda shot out at full speed under the cover of withering fire. Once they had crossed half the distance to the large enemy ship, the Waratah was flung out of the Matilda's hangar bay by the catapult system.

"Woo!" Luli blasted over the open comms.

"Be nice to my ship, Lu! Not a scratch! You promised!" shouted Derain.

"Not a scratch!" Luli's laugh rang loudly over the comm.

"Remember, Waratah, we have seven hours before they nuke the planet. Be at the rendezvous... please." Jacquie switched off the comm. "I keyed in the coordinates for the last held position of the ground forces before they lost contact in the nav system. Get us there as fast as you can."

"Got it, Captain." Anton angled the Matilda toward Ninguiz. "We should break atmo in twenty."

"Derain, have you found that beacon?" asked Jacquie.

He acknowledged, "Nothing yet, but it's on the far side of that rock."

The Matilda broke through the cloud layer to find a barren and rocky planet. As the ship cruised closer to the surface, Derain was able to just barely pick up the weak beacon. Anton altered the trajectory and headed straight for it. The beacon's signal came from the center of the ruins of what once had been a small city. No movement was visible, but fires still smoldered throughout the rubble when Anton set the ship down. He landed the Matilda in a clearing that was only a short distance from the beacon.

Derain informed everyone on board, "I'm not getting a radio response from the frequency the Remus gave us. Going in blind to a war zone might be unwise."

"There is rarely any other way, Derain," groused Anton.

"Let's keep our profile to a minimum then. Get the cloak on." Jacquie commed to Barney,

"Meet us at the cargo bay. Be ready for trouble."

"Got it."

"Pretty quiet out there. Keep an eye out, Rabbit. Derain you're with me." Jacquie exited the bridge.

"Stay safe," Anton shot back.

***

Luli kicked in the attitude jets to pull up before she slammed into the remains of a broken ship. The Waratah spun after clearing it to avoid the damaged vessel that took up most of the view in the bow port. Blaster fire erupted all around the craft as Luli made for the gigantic ship that hung suspended in the center of the rift. "Do you see an airlock or the hangar bay for that thing?"

"To the port side, up top; looks like a big opening," answered Galena. "Thanks for coming with me, Luli. I am indebted."

"I see it. That tin can of a ship is torn up!" Luli glanced toward Galena, "I couldn't let you go by yourself. I still have to teach you how to dance!" She laughed maniacally, "Damn I love to fly like this!"

The Waratah cut tightly alongside the large ship. Luli slammed the attitude jets to cut downwards and slid into the open hangar bay. Wreckage lay everywhere. A human body slapped into the bow port as she cut the jets to bring the ship to a relative halt. Galena fired the boarding harpoons to keep the ship from floating free in the gutted hangar bay. The two women nodded to each other as they unbuckled from their seats and floated to the hatch.

"The grav is dead in there, so at least this thing won't weigh much," Luli remarked.

Galena nodded and grabbed one end of the bomb. Luli triggered the hatch and then grabbed the other end of the explosive. Loaded for bear, the two of them floated out into the ravaged hangar bay and made their way to the blown hatch that led toward the interior of the ship.

***

"Do you see anyone?" Jacquie shouted into the dry wind. She registered the negative head shake from Derain and waited while Barney zeroed in on the beacon with his scanner. He pointed to his left, then headed off in that direction. Jacquie turned toward the spot where the Matilda should have been, but there was an emptiness in its place; an emptiness with a light glimmer on the edge of her vision. "Seems to work pretty well, even up close."

"What seems to work pretty well?" asked a female voice behind her as she felt the tip of a barrel press into the back of her neck.

"Oh, you know, my undeniable magnetism." Jacquie sensed her pistol being withdrawn from her shoulder holster as the barrel tip crept down to the middle of her back and pushed her forward.

"I can tell that you want to strike at me. I would suggest that you do not," the voice continued behind her. "Follow your small ally, please."

"What? Me move? Why should I? I am feeling very comfortable." Jacquie slowed her steps, "I don't know what small ally you're talking about. Are you sure you saw one?" She looked over her shoulder and faltered, "What the...?"

The woman standing behind her monitored the movement and struck Jacquie in the back of the skull. The Captain crumpled to the ground in a heap. "Soldier Delta 555-74K requesting assistance with prisoner," the genorg asked into her comm.

Derain watched from a distance as the female drone, just like their Lieutenant, picked up Jacquie's body and threw it over her shoulder. Another female drone came up beside her and the two of them walked in the same direction Barney had gone. "I thought the Lieutenant was a one off for soldiering?" He adjusted his refraction coat settings. He disappeared into the surroundings and then silently followed after them.

***

Luli wiped at a corroded name plate that she had discovered in the latest of long hallways that stretched before them, "The Avadora. Looks like an old cruise liner, although I don't recognize the style. Do you?"

"I wouldn't know a ship manufacturer from a door knob maker," muttered Galena as she held onto one end of the bomb. "It's a very nice ship, but will you hurry up and figure out where we need to go?"

"Just a minute!" Luli scanned for the power source that must be keeping the gateway open. "I don't think we've crossed the threshold yet." She turned to the Lieutenant, "We'll have to go further in."

Luli floated down the hallway with Galena in tow. They coasted through an intersection and came across their first living person, though living might be a relative term. The body jerked spasmodically while some sort of viscous fluid ebbed and flowed through the broken faceplate. Luli gulped and double checked her life sign readings to make certain they were as low as she could keep them. She grabbed a handhold on the walls to propel them and their cargo further along. Galena kept them steady as they floated onward toward their goal. As they continued through the ship, they came across other living bodies. Some would just float there and vibrate; others writhed in various unnatural poses. But there was a sameness to them; same suit, same build.

"Is it just me or are all of them women?"

Jon Gray Lang

"It's not just you," Galena swallowed as she was able to make out a partial face through the broken faceplate. "They are all my sisters." She looked away as they passed the lower half of a body torn in two.

Luli felt sick at the thought of what Galena must be going through. Her scanner beeped and then it beeped again. "I'm finally getting a reading. We must be past the threshold now."

***

Derain followed the two women through the ruins. The signs of battle were everywhere. Broken bodies lay strewn throughout the rocks and strangely, most of the bodies were of the same drone model. Many of the corpses had been decapitated.

The two women walked past the beacon that had brought the Matilda here and finally entered a hovel built out of rubble. There were many more of the genorg females inside and around the base camp. Most of them were filthy and in poor condition, wounded or ill.

Derain took up a position where he could keep an eye on the camp and made a note of where they placed Jacquie. He watched as another of the genorg troops came by and dropped Barney next to her. They both spluttered awake and looked wildly around after getting a face full of what-one-hoped, was water. The drone that had carried

Jacquie here stared at the two of them until they stopped searching for an escape route. Another genorg whispered something into her ear and then stepped to the side.

"I am Soldier Delta 555-74K. Soldier Gamma 768-32Y tells me that both of you are clean. Neither of you are infected." She turned her eyes to Jacquie, "Explain your purpose here," she indicated all around, "And your roll in this campaign."

Jacquie opened her mouth to speak when suddenly Anton's voice rang out from Derain's hiding place, "Have you guys made contact yet? Hello?"

***

Luli's scanner had taken them deep into the bowels of the ship. Once past the threshold, the hallways of the Avadora extended into what appeared to be infinity. The decking took on strange proportions and seemed to undulate beneath their feet. The bomb itself had taken on a lot more weight and they became aware of a sickly sweet stench of grapefruit and old blood that was overwhelming. The walls stretched and folded in on themselves; some felt soft to the touch when they rippled over the two women.

The forces of gravity within the ship warped the further they went in. They encountered fewer of Galena's sisters, but the ones they did pass moved aside of their own accord. The genorgs would stare blankly at the two women as they walked by, their eyes black to the edges of the skin of their sockets. Due to Luli's lack of a body temperature, the drones regarded her as nothing more than a machine. However, once they registered Galena, they would ignore the two women as if they didn't exist and go back about their business.

As the two journeyed deeper into the ship, the walls looked like melted candles and bizarre creatures the size of a human child became more prevalent. These poor beasts suffered in their movements as their bodily proportions were ungainly in the minor gravity. Their appearance was hard to look upon. It was as if a mad god had assembled them from an immense pile of spare parts.

The interior of the ship took on a more industrial look as they stumbled onto the lower service decks. Wispy coral like plants and glowing fungi grew out of the walls here and they undulated. The feeling that the entire ship was breathing was hard to ignore. The scanner on Luli's HUD suddenly emitted a stronger location beacon for the power source of the rift.

"We're close, Lieutenant." Luli gestured toward the paneling, "If this ship can hold its internal shape for any amount of time, I'd say we've got a couple decks to go down and to the port side." She glanced around at the pulsating walls, "But in this case? Who knows?"

"This seems curiously familiar..."

whispered Galena. She turned suddenly and headed for a partially obscured lift, "It's this way..."

"I'm glad someone here has a clue where we're going..." Luli muttered.

***

Barney watched as clusters of the genorgs took off toward what looked like empty landscape, only to have Derain appear as if by magic. "I forgot he had one of those." He turned to Jacquie, "Hey, we need more of those. Especially one for me. The rest of you can wait." He glared at the closest genorg, "I get the first one, because, I am getting tired of being hit on the head. Tired of it!"

They brought Derain down into the camp. He was pushed down roughly, right next to Barney.

He muttered, "I am going to kill that man."

"You and me both," Jacquie remarked.

The soldier Delta came to stand in front of the three of them, "I still require an answer. What is your purpose here?"

Jacquie sized her up, "Well, we were going to rescue the lot of you, but I am seriously rethinking that option."

The genorg looked questioningly, "Rescue? Why?"

Barney screamed out, "Because your

benefactors are going to turn this planet into glass!"

"But we are expendable. What purpose is served by our leaving?" wondered Soldier Gamma.

"Well, your continuation to be expendable, for one," he articulated.

"You're wasting your time, Barney. These drones aren't as enlightened as our Lieutenant," Derain observed.

Barney glared at him, "You are not helping." He turned back to the genorgs, "There is more to life than just war, you know. Don't you want to experience other things? Don't you want your... uh... sisters to stay alive? Do their lives mean so little to you?"

"We serve to live and live to..." the soldiers repeated together as a mantra.

"...to serve. Yeah, yeah I've heard Galena spout that line of crap before," Jacquie interrupted.

The genorgs perked up at the mention of her name. They came from all around and formed a circle around Jacquie. Questions bubbled up from the group, "You know the First Soldier?" "Is she here?" "Can we meet her?" "Where is she?"

Delta raised her hand to silence the others and stared pointedly at the Captain. Just as she opened her mouth, Jacquie answered the questions she had heard. "The Lieutenant is part of my crew and she is in this system. Right now, she is trying to save everyone's collective ass up there," she said, looking up toward the sky.

The drones waited for their leader to respond. Eventually the one who had introduced herself as Gamma spoke quizzically, "She is trying to save us?"

Barney broke in, "You, me, your leaders and anyone left in this rat hole of a planetary system."

"There is no saving the infected," declared Delta. "Does the First Soldier desire us to be rescued?"

With half lidded eyes, Jacquie spat out each word, "Yes. She does. So, can we get a move on?"

***

Galena no longer felt distracted as she launched herself down the lift, literally dragging Luli behind her. She landed lightly on her toes two decks below and launched herself down the hallway that sprawled in front of her. The ship's artificial gravity barely functioned and Luli was pulled off her feet. The Lieutenant ignored her as she floated toward her destination.

Luli regained her feet and realized that they were still headed toward the Engine Room. The 'otherness' of this dimension leaked through the gashes left in the hallway paneling that had puddled to the decking. The framing of the ship stood out like the bones of a rotting carcass. Mold in a spectrum of unknown colors covered the remnants of the decking. Abominations crawled around and through the girders of the decking below her feet. These were larger and some grew from the corpses of what Luli could only assume had once been the crew of this long dead ship. She was glad that the artificial gravity was broken here.

The hatch to the Engine Room was gone. The rents left from the hinges that had been ripped from the walls stood out in stark contrast to the sickness of the rot that grew everywhere. They entered the Engine Room and the stench of burnt copper and rotting vegetation brought Luli to her knees. Galena seemed unaffected, though. The Lieutenant dropped her end of the bomb and landed in front of a huge coalescing ball of light in a cradle in the center of the room. Luli regained her feet and watched Galena stare blankly at what was reminiscent of a much larger version of the jump engine on board the Matilda.

"Oh my," she stammered. "I have got to get some readings of this thing for Barney or he'll never forgive me. Can you set the timer on the explosive?" She turned to the Lieutenant, "Galena? Are you listening?"

Galena turned slowly in her direction; her feet barely touched the deck plates. Her voice sounded as if it came from a great distance, "Yes? Yes... I can do that... timers..." She grabbed her end of the bomb case and dragged it over to the cradle that held the engine. She dropped to her knees, opened the lid and flipped the switch to open the timer panel. She keyed the controls, but her eyes kept shifting to stare deeply into the jump engine.

Luli stood next to the jump engine and had her scanners pull as much information as possible from it. She barely noticed Galena as she dragged the bomb closer to her. Fluctuating color patterns that played on the surface of the mechanism reflected on her faceplate and she froze in their light. Luli discerned a repeating pattern and documented it. Suddenly, a guttural scream pierced the silent room.

A monstrous grub-like creature smashed through the open hatch followed by a multitude of freaks of nature in a miscellany of proportions and forms. Galena's scream tore through the helmet comm as she pulled her pistol and fired repeatedly into the behemoth. Luli unholstered her weapon, leapt to the side and sprayed rounds into the pack of beasts as they burst into the room. Galena's scream stopped abruptly when the worm reared up and swallowed her from the shoulders up.

"No!" shouted Luli.

She holstered her empty pistol and grabbed a rusted spanner lying on the deck. Leaping toward the gigantic wormlike beast, she struck it repeatedly with the tool. She moved nimbly out of the way of Galena's gun blasts as she shot indiscriminately into the body of the monster. The worm shuddered and arched back as black, viscous liquid splattered from the impacts. Galena's helmet, covered in this same black viscous goo, slipped free of the monster's grasp.

Audible screams emitted from the partially obscured mouth of the Lieutenant and she shook where she stood. Her cries petered out and she toppled forward to lie on the deck, unmoving. Luli leapt free of the dying worm and faced the remaining creatures in the room. However, they had lost all interest once Galena had fallen and they squirmed their way out of the engine room.

Luli dropped the spanner and ran over to Galena, "Lieutenant! You there, Lieutenant?" She shook her, but there was no response. She checked the vitals readout on Galena's suit; she was still alive. The suit registered a heartbeat, but it fluttered weakly.

"Damn it!" Luli pulled at the ooze that had ripped a hole through the genorg's faceplate, and it slithered away of its own volition. Her hands dropped to her sides in frustration.

"First things first," she growled.

She strode over to the bomb, quickly keyed through the remaining timer settings and slammed the lid closed. She put her hands on her hips and stared at her friend's body lying on the deck.

"Looks like I get to carry you back," she muttered.

***

It had not taken as long as Jacquie had expected to get the planet's survivors organized enough to move toward the Matilda. A total of three hundred eighty nine of the genorg troops were still alive. However, the personnel carriers were only designed to hold one hundred fifty people each, in relative comfort. It would be a tight fit. The sickbay would be overloaded. It would require luck and some ingenuity to get all of the survivors off this death trap of a planet, but it could be done.

Anton brought the Matilda's cloaking device down and the remnants of the Consortium ground forces approached with Jacquie in the lead. Barney directed the soldiers to place the most grievously wounded into the med lab. He had the less severe cases placed in the available med tubes until Doc was able to get to them. The rest of the genorg troops were marched up to the main shaft and seated in the two personnel carrier containers.

Jacquie waited with Derain in the cargo bay as the soldiers stood in precise lines for their turn to enter the lift.

"I've got to say, these drones are pretty well organized. This is going much smoother than I would have anticipated," Derain told her.

"From what I gather, I don't think they know much else. Marching in line and war is all the training they've received. It is a little uncanny though."

Gun fire erupted outside the ship. Orders were shouted by the soldier drones and a defensive line was quickly created beyond the open cargo bay. Derain pulled his pistol and headed out to check on the situation. Jacquie took up a defensive position along the inner door.

He returned pretty quickly, "Looks like the locals of this ball and more of the drone soldiers are attacking us, but they all appear to be unhealthy, almost distorted. They look... twisted." He turned back to the open doors of the cargo bay, "The soldiers mentioned an infestation, right? I'm thinking that's what happened to those out there. We need to speed this up."

Jacquie keyed up to the bridge, "Hey Anton, throw some suppression fire out there. We still have about a company left to get on board."

"Aye, aye Captain."

"Delta! Pull your people back!" Jacquie ordered.

Derain and Jacquie provided cover fire for the soldiers as one of the coil guns on the Matilda dug a huge furrow through the hillside and atomized the attackers. The ship shook again as another coil gun blast ripped through a new section of the hillside.

"That do the trick, Captain?" Anton's voice smirked through the comm.

"I love a man who knows how to use a big gun... especially if it's mine," she joked.

"Uh... right."

Derain just chuckled.

Soldier Gamma came over and gazed at the bounty hunter quizzically, but she addressed Jacquie, "Please come." She turned and walked back out of the ship.

"I guess I'll be going that way. Hold her down for me, would you?" She followed the genorg out.

"As you wish," Derain answered, watching her walk away.

"Captain, please follow me," Delta requested as Jacquie met up with her. The genorg headed toward the closest body of one of the attackers, a local inhabitant who was still alive, although both of his legs were broken. She pointed at the body, "As you can see, this one is contaminated. If any of us show signs of infection while on board your ship, we must be exterminated immediately." She paused a moment to let that sink in, "There is no surviving it, there is no other option."

***

With Galena strapped across her body, Luli finally located the lift they had come down in. She launched herself up the shaft and leapt out the lift doorway that her internal map listed as the right floor... even though it was three floors up and she only remembered having gone two floors down. The ship had altered even more in the short time it had taken them to get to the Engine Room. The accuracy of her internal map was now even less than when they had entered. She had to backtrack a few times and guess at which routes might be correct.

She passed a familiar tangle of the creatures in her pursuit for escape and they had grown larger since her first encounter with them. The beasts showed less interest in her passing now and she was very thankful for that. The timer on the bomb had been set with a mapped exit route and this return journey was taking far longer than it should.

"I hope things are more normal past the threshold, I really do," she mumbled out loud. A wispy plantlike organism turned in her direction, but flowed back into the current that controlled its movements. "I'm not talking to you."

***

Jacquie stared down at the squirming body and could see what Derain had meant. The features were elongated and the skin looked rough, almost ashen in color. The eyes were entirely black and devoid of any sign of intelligence.

Delta drew her pistol and shot it through the head. A thick viscous fluid leaked from the exit wound. "We lost entire squads to the infection and this is the only solution. The change is quick, only hours." She holstered her pistol and headed back to the ship, "I need you to understand the severity of the situation. We need to hurry, because they will be back. They do not stop."

Jacquie felt sick to her stomach. She had seen plenty of horrible things throughout her life, but nothing that equaled this. "How much longer do you think it will take to get everyone aboard?"

"Within a half hour. If you are willing to launch and sort it out in the air, about five minutes."

"Five minutes it is."

The soldiers piled on board the ship and searched for any place to strap into. A screech erupted in the distance as the contaminated swarmed over the hillside. The deck of the Matilda rumbled and another coil gun projectile tore through the advancing attackers, but this time it didn't slow them. They continued to swarm toward the ship. Derain took pot shots until the cargo bay doors shut and the Matilda launched.

The hull reverberated from hand held rocket fire, but the Matilda had been built to withstand such small arms. She was essentially a flying tank. The ship came about in a full circle and burnt the closest of the infected to dust. Anton poured on the afterburners and shot up to break the planet's atmosphere.

Jacquie stumbled onto the bridge through the turbulence and grabbed the communications station. She keyed over to the CBC

Remus, "Zeus! We are free of the planet's gravity well. I say again, we are free of the planet's gravity well." She keyed the comm off and squeezed Anton's shoulder, "They can fire those nukes at any time. Any word from the Waratah?"

"Nothing yet..."

***

Luli had been right and she was exceptionally glad for it. Once she passed the threshold point, the ship retained most of its internal structure. The living drones on this side of the rift barely moved or acknowledged her passing.

"Should be a straight run to the hangar bay and then we're outta here, Galena. You just hang on, alright?"

Galena's body remained mute though she could feel it twitching against her chassis. The gravity weakened once she passed the threshold. She half ran, half floated as quickly as possible down the hallways, back toward the hangar bay. The strange plant life had begun to grow on this side of the ship as well, but in comparison to the other half of the ship, it was still quite sparse.

Luli released a pent up breath when she reached the blown hatch to the hangar bay. She spied the Waratah as it floated serenely in the open space, held in place by the tethers. She looked over her shoulder at Galena's face. The blackish fluid had hardened somewhat, but Luli could still see her mouth through the broken faceplate. The atmosphere in the Avadora had been light, but there wasn't any atmosphere at all in the hangar bay or in the Waratah.

"This is it, Lieutenant! I need you to hang on a little while longer, Okay? Just stay alive enough, so we can revive you. Got it?" She turned back toward the hangar bay, "Alive enough so that you don't have brain damage, too. Hear that, Major Tom? I'm calling on you."

Luli sucked in a breath, angled herself for a clean trajectory to their ship and launched. Like a missile with a passenger strapped to it, they flew in a straight line toward the Waratah. Luli spied stirrings from some of the bodies that floated in the bay. A few of them turned at her passing and one that had purchase launched itself after her.

"I don't have time for this!"

She drew the Lieutenant's pistol and fired at the one following them. Another one began moving toward her and she blasted a hole through its head. She grabbed the closest handhold on the Waratah and pulled up to the hatch. Luli looked over her shoulder as she keyed in the entrance code. The hatch popped just as she turned to push a drone away from her.

She lifted the hatch, hopped in and dropped the strap that held the Lieutenant to her. She keyed the lock to the hatch and felt the slight pressure change. Something thumped against the hull.

She checked the timer she had set for the explosion, "Just enough..."

Luli grabbed Galena, strapped her into the copilot's seat and belted herself into the pilot's chair. A man slapped into the bow port, which caused her to jump. He futilely scrabbled for handholds against the surface as his dead eyes tracked Luli's movements. She thumbed through the commands to bring the ship on line at a speed only a cyborg could manage. When the engines kicked, she cut the tethers and spun the craft on its axis. The ship's close combat weapons automatically opened fire and ripped the attackers into shreds. She spun the Waratah around and launched it out of the Avadora's hangar bay at full throttle.

"I'm glad we're blowing that tin can," she cried. "Good riddance!" Galena's body twitched in the straps that held her in the copilot seat.

***

Anton spoke to the Captain, "I'm getting a weak transponder signal from the Waratah. She appears to be on the move."

Jacquie cried in relief, "Finally. Hail Luli and tell her to get aboard as soon as they can." She turned to Derain, "Have we gotten our guests stowed for the voyage?"

"They are loading the last of the survivors into seats now. We'll have about twenty

THE MATILDA **307**

outside of the carrier containers, not including those in the med lab. Should we have them bunk in the lounge?"

"Let's keep them off top deck for now. There's plenty of room in the cargo bay."

"Did we get any instructions from the CBC Captain on what to do with them or where to drop them off?" Anton asked.

Luli's voice erupted on the ship to ship comm, "Waratah to Matilda... Waratah to Matilda... please respond!"

Anton switched to the active channel, "Matilda to Waratah, we read you. Glad to hear your voice, Lu!"

"... I repeat, the Lieutenant is down. Have a tube ready for her, we're coming in hot!"

Anton planned the two trajectories on the nav system, "Meet at 901-mark-7!"

***

"Be there in the shake of a rabbit's tail. Waratah out." Luli looked over at Galena's body as it floated against the straps in the copilot seat. "We'll get that stuff cleaned off you... we will," she promised.

The black viscous fluid swirled back and forth through the hole in her faceplate as if it were alive.

***

Jon Gray Lang

Captain Kaplean's ship entered the Pequiz system under its own FTL drive; since the received orders had stated Full Evacuation Protocol would be in place for the system's gate. He scowled as the full impact of the traffic at the jump gate lit up the bow port. "We still came in too close, Grissom. Please, move us out with all haste."

A ship rammed into one of the jump gate generators, which set off an explosion. That ship spun out of control from the blast and slammed into another one. Like a child with dominoes, ship after ship slammed together, each one reverberating outward to crash into another one. With the loss of the generator, the jump gate went dark.

"Lieutenant Hayley, get a repair team sent to the gate." The Captain keyed the comm, "Chief, get some of our birds out there to organize this mess." He switched to the full ship's comm, "We are en route to Ninguiz. Everyone man your battle stations!"

Lieutenant Hayley responded, "Repair team is away sir. I am in communication with the CBC Remus. They are asking why another ship has been dispatched."

"What other ship? More detail please."

"Requesting more detail, sir."

The ship cruised quickly toward Ninguiz until the bridge crew could see the rent in the blackness of space. It pulsated like the heartbeat of some enormous alien being. An eerie hush spread across the bridge as they all stared at it. The Consortium fleet was still engaged in battle when two streaks shot from it toward the surface of the planet.

"Sir!" blurted the technician, "I am getting a configuration match for the cargo hauler we lost in the Spur system!"

"Track that ship, Cordelan," Captain Kaplean ordered. "How much further to our rendezvous, Grissom?"

Lieutenant Hayley reported, "Captain Ellsbeth says the warheads are en route to the planet's surface. The soldier in charge of destroying the enemy ship was a Lieutenant Chadov?"

"We should be there inside of three minutes, sir," replied Navigation Officer Grissom.

A brilliant burst of light lit up the center of the tear in space followed by two flashes on the planet's surface. The bridge crew had to shield their eyes from the blasts as the port plas-glass couldn't react fast enough to reduce the brilliance of the light.

Scanner Technician Cordelan cleared his eyes and checked the tracking report on the strange ship. He grimaced and said flatly, "We lost her Captain. She jumped away."

Captain Kaplean stared out the bow port in silence as the plas-glass cleared to its standard settings and the roiling destruction became visible in the light of the system's sun. "Gone again." He keyed the comm to Doctor Wyeth's cabin, "Doctor, we just lost your Lieutenant Chadov. She announced herself to the Captain of the CBC Remus. We are en route to gather intel."

"Excellent, Captain," Doctor Wyeth replied. "I am glad you were finally able to make some headway in this. So far, Galena Chadov is the only one who has survived contact with those beasts. And we need to find out why."

thirty-three

The Songs for the Chapter Titles

In case you didn't notice, all the chapter names are actually song titles and they are supposed to be part of Ms. Luli Qing's performances. These songs helped me put together the various chapters but in some cases only certain versions were used. If you were interested, here they are:

- ☐ Boney was a Warrior - Old Folk Song
- ☐ We're Bound for Botany Bay - Old Folk Song
- ☐ The Dead Horse Shanty - Old Folk Song
- ☐ Spanish Ladies - Old Folk Song
- ☐ Whiskey in the Jar - Old Folk Song
- ☐ Born Under a Bad Sign - Albert King
- ☐ Nobody's Fault but Mine - Blind Willie Johnson
- ☐ Keep on Moving - Bob Marley

Jon Gray Lang

- ☐ Ghost Riders in the Sky - Johnny Cash
- ☐ Straighten Up and Fly Right - Nat King Cole
- ☐ Beauty and Stupid - Hide
- ☐ Rebel, Rebel - David Bowie
- ☐ All The Rockets Go Bang - Bob Log III
- ☐ Life on Mars - David Bowie
- ☐ Running Home - Reuben Halsey
- ☐ Fly Me to the Moon - Frank Sinatra
- ☐ Spin, Spin, Sugar - Sneaker Pimps
- ☐ Danse Russe - Hurt
- ☐ Jimmy, Jimmy - The Undertones
- ☐ One Whole Hour - Scarlett Johannson
- ☐ Turkey in the Straw - Old Folk Song
- ☐ Sixteen Tons – Tennessee Ernie Ford
- ☐ Sinner Man - Nina Simone
- ☐ Blister in the Sun - Violent Femmes
- ☐ Tomorrow Never Knows - The Beatles
- ☐ Black Hole Sun - Sound Garden
- ☐ The New Order - Testament
- ☐ Two Against One - Jack White
- ☐ Lead Sails (And a Paper Anchor) - Atreyu
- ☐ Corona - Minutemen
- ☐ Diggin' My Grave - William Elliot Whitmore
- ☐ Streets of Laredo - Marty Robbins

The title of the book is also a song:
- ☐ Matilda - Alt-J

Jon Gray Lang

I hope you enjoyed hanging out with the crew of the Matilda. The Matilda's story continues in Twistin' Matilda!

Jon Gray Lang

***

Check out a Sneak Peak of *Nun With a Gun* below!

Dark secrets plagued the Town with No Name, and fear lived in the hearts of its people.

That was before the nun appeared on the horizon like a mirage on a hot, sunny day. A well-used pistol swung from her hip while a rosary crucifix dangled loosely from her closed fist. She came with no horse, no wagon, and no donkey. Only the two legs given by the Lord propelled her into our little desert home.

But was she here to save us, or was she here to bring justice to those that deserve it?

Jon Gray Lang

Arrival

She appeared on the horizon like a mirage on a hot, sunny day. She came with no horse, no wagon, and no donkey. Only the two legs the Lord gave her propelled her into our little town.

She wore the colors of black and white as if they were branded into her skin. Her habit shadowed her face while her skirt billowed around her. Her bright eyes were sharp, like a hawk. Many an eye turned at her passing down the dusty street. Many an evil man cowered under that gaze as she passed them by.

About her waist hung a gun belt. Well-worn was the leather and the steel of the Colt Peacemaker gleamed in the sun. From one wrist dangled a string of prayer beads made of darkest ebony. A single cross hung at the end, and it swayed with the movement from her steps.

She read the signs emblazoned above each business on our main street as she passed them by. The Feed Store, The Bank, and others were left in her wake. She came to a stop in front of the only

Jon Gray Lang

saloon left in our dying town, The Bronze Dogie.

She pushed through the grimy saloon doors and into the darkened interior. The place reeked of tobacco smoke, sweat-stained bodies, and the effects of too much liquor. She peered at the bleary faces as they stared back at her. With a slow, practiced motion, she swept the road dust from her habit until it reflected in the dim lighting.

The left saloon door swayed from her passing until the hinge broke and it clattered loudly to the wooden flooring.

***

About the Author

Jon Gray Lang was born in Australia before being hastily relocated to the United States where he wrote a handful of screenplays, shot a few films, and even threw his hat into the acting ring. But with a life-long love of science fiction, it was only a matter of time before he bit the novel writing bullet and wrote the award-winning five book science fiction series, Saga of a Space Freighter. When he's not typing away at the keyboard, he's busy fighting with rapiers, skiing the Rockies, or banging out tunes on a ukulele... just not all at once... No matter how hard he tries.

Please follow him on:
JonGrayLang.com
facebook.com/JonGrayLang
twitter.com/Jon_Gray_Lang
instagram.com/jongraylang

<<<<>>>>

Jon Gray Lang

www.ingramcontent.com/pod-product-compliance
Lightning Source LLC
Chambersburg PA
CBHW030645260626
47157CB00007B/2507